BEAUTY'S BEAST

STASIA BLACK
LEE SAVINO

Copyright © 2020 by Stasia Black and Lee Savino

All rights reserved. No part of this publication may be reproduced, distributed, or transmitted in any form or by any means, including photocopying, recording, or other electronic or mechanical methods, without the prior written permission of the publisher, except in the case of brief quotations embodied in critical reviews and certain other noncommercial uses permitted by copyright law.

This is a work of fiction. Similarities to real people, places, or events are entirely coincidental.

ISBN-13: 978-1-950097-68-5

Cover design by Jay Aheer

PROLOGUE

THE BEAST LOOMS OVER ME, half in shadow. In the dark, the scarred skin around his mask disappears. When he turns his head I get a sense of deja vu, like I know him from somewhere—

"Go to the bed and lie down, face up," he demands.

I swallow. My hands come up automatically to cover my breasts. "Ah ah," he catches my wrists and moves them apart, baring my chest to his gaze. My heart is pounding, overwhelmed. I'm so vulnerable right now.

Still holding my wrists, he backs me to the bed. When he lets go, I scramble up and lay back. Maybe if I obey him, I won't have to worry. I won't have to think. Let go and be mine, he said earlier. But can I really do that? This man is my enemy.

And yet, when I see him rise after bending to grab something at the base of the bed, I scuttle to the headboard and plant myself there, my knees drawn up to my chest.

"You want to tie me up?" I squeak. "Again?"

He tosses the chain onto the bed. The silver length has a leather cuff on the end. I clutch my wrist.

His gaze never leaving mine, he heads to the foot of the bed, leans down, and reveals a second restraint. There's one at each corner of the bed. Holy—

He ends up beside me again, unbuckling the leather cuff for my left wrist.

"Submit, Daphne."

Run. Any sane woman would run. I'm out of my mind, giving into this...craving this. It's wrong. All of this, so so wrong. I could tell myself I have no choice, but it's not true.

I could've protested when he announced it was time for my punishment, and he would've backed down, tucked me into bed and coddled me like an invalid. It was my curiosity as much as his depravity spurring us forward. I don't want to stop. I'm in too deep.

So I scoot down and lie back. After a pause, I slowly spread my arms and legs. The ultimate submission. That fact that the position makes my pussy throb has nothing to do with it. How long will I keep lying to myself about why I'm really staying?

"Good girl," he murmurs, taking my left arm and securing the cuff around my wrist. "Flex your fingers for me?" I do and he strokes the tips. His dark eyes bore into mine and my core clenches. He only has to touch my fingertips to turn me on.

"Too tight?" he asks. My breath hitches and I shake my head. His cheek curls—another smile!—and he heads down to cuff my feet.

"You're being so good, Daphne. You know what that means?"

"What?" My voice is husky. The sound of it surprises me—I've turned into a sexpot. I've never felt like this before, but this moment is one of many firsts. He's still dressed like always, but this time, I'm unafraid as he strips me bare.

Lying down and letting him restrain me with an excited willingness.

I've never been more turned on. My nipples are crinkled peaks, begging for attention.

"It means you get a reward." He turns and walks away, leaving me helpless and bound. My arms are stretched over my head, my legs able to bend a little but not move much more than that. What is he going to do to me?

When he returns, I'm almost panting, my heart fluttering in the cage of my chest like a captured bird. But my nipples are harder than ever. And my pussy aches...

"Shhhh." He lays a large hand on my chest, splayed over my breastbone. "Calm, Daphne. I won't hurt you." A quirk of his lips, a crooked smile. "At least, not more than you like. Because you like some pain, don't you, kitten?"

He leans in and breathes in my ear, drenching my sex with his every word. "There's so much for us to explore. So many combinations of pain and pleasure. So many ways to make you feel alive..." He lowers himself down and I let my head fall back. I can't fight anymore. When his tongue finally touches me, I give in completely.

ONE

Daphne

I SCRUB my eyes as I jog up the stairs after another exhaustive session down in the lab. Still no breakthroughs.

I circle around to my desk. Maybe if I just resequence the—

But then I freeze.

A single red rose is waiting for me on my computer keyboard. I approach my desk carefully, looking around.

But there's no one in this part of the building. No secretary or gatekeeper to witness a random rose delivery. Nothing but the normal hum of machines from the offices down the hall.

Except for the rose.

My desk looks the same—stacks of paper, lab reports in white binders, budget reports in green ones. My stomach gives a growl. I haven't eaten anything but a granola bar at some point during the night. What time *is* it? I've been down in the lab for who knows how long. It's easy to lose track of time down there.

My hunger can wait. I circle my desk and settle into my chair, leaning down to study the rose as if it's something other than a pretty blossom—something dangerous, like a bomb.

But it's just a rose. There's no note, no hint of who sent it.

Just like last year, and the year before, and every year since my eighteenth birthday.

I roll the stem between my thumb and forefinger. When I can't wait any longer, I bring the bright red bloom to my face and drink in the sweet perfume.

Most store-bought roses have no scent. They've been bred over the years for appearance instead of fragrance. But this rose is different.

This rose grew in a garden.

"*Rosa x hybrida,*" I murmur the Latin name. The thick rosette petals are like a fancy lady's ball gown and petticoats. Definitely a hybrid bloom.

"Daphne?" my assistant Rachel calls.

"In here," I call, without pulling the rose from my face.

"How did I know I'd find you here or down in your hermit hole?" Rachel walks in, her eyes glued to her tablet. In her white skirt suit with her blonde hair in an elegant chignon, she looks more like a CEO than I do. The pen tucked behind her ear only makes her more official.

"Okay, because I know you won't let it rest till I update you, I sent the board the updated merger packet, but I still need—" She finally looks up and stops talking when she sees me pressing the rose to my face. "Is that...?"

I nod.

Her posture softens, her face registering sympathy.

She's one of the few people who knows about the mysterious yearly rose delivery and the event it marks. "Oh, Daphne. Is it today? I thought it was last week."

"No, you're right, it was Wednesday. You arranged the bouquet to be delivered, right?" I must look ridiculous, sitting at my desk in my lab coat, sniffing a rose. I briskly stack a few papers on my desk.

Rachel nods. "A dozen white roses. I had them delivered directly to Thornhill. Are you going to visit?"

"Not this year." It hurts to even say it. Who doesn't have time to go visit their own mother's grave? I tap the desk, my fingers itching to pick up the rose again. I grab a tiny origami swan off my desk instead—a gift from one of the many Battleman's patients who are counting on my research.

"I don't have time. I would've gone Wednesday, but I had to prepare for the meeting with the board. I'm already on thin ice with them."

Not that the meeting went well.

"What time is it?" I change the subject. My eyes are too tired to check a clock.

"Three in the afternoon. On Saturday."

"What?" I whip off my glasses and grind the heel of my free hand into my eye socket, trying to get rid of the gritty feeling. "Really? When did that happen?"

"It's a result of the earth rotating combined with its position relative to the sun." Her tone is perfectly dry. "Happens approximately every twenty-four hours." She crosses her arms over her chest. "You promised me you would stop working through the night."

"I wanted to put the results of my latest experiment into a report for the board. Show them how much progress we've made..."

"Daphne, you can't keep doing this. I know you're a genius and all, but you're not Super Woman."

"I slept a little. I think." I stretch my neck to the side and rotate my shoulder. My muscles creak and crunch in protest. Pretty sad for a twenty-six year, almost twenty-seven year old. "And I'm not a genius."

Rachel snorts.

I narrow my eyes at her. "Wait, if it's Saturday, why are you here?"

"To get you ready."

I yawn and stretch my arms above my head. "Ready for what?"

She raises a brow. "The Autumn Gala."

I groan and let my head fall back on my chair. "Oh shit, that's tonight. I completely forgot."

"You're going through a lot." She picks up an old newspaper off my desk and makes a face at it before tossing it into the trash. "I wouldn't bug you about this but—"

"No, no, I'm glad you're bugging me. I have to go to the gala."

"Donations from the Ubeli foundation are still a significant part of our R&D budget," Rachel recites. "Without the Ubeli's generosity, Belladonna would've shut down year one."

"I know, I know." I stand and stretch. "I've been going to these since I was a teen." A gangly, awkward girl, out of her depth among the glamour and glitter of the highest echelons of New Olympus society.

Ten years hasn't changed much. I'm taller. And still can't wear heels for shit. "Oh gods, how am I going to get through this?"

"It'll be fine. Cora Ubeli likes you."

"Cora Ubeli is the supreme ruler of high society. She'll

be surrounded by people. And I usually go there with Dad." This is the first year I'll be alone.

Rachel picks up the rose and toys with it. "Maybe you'll meet..." she deepens her voice playfully. "your secret admirer."

"I do not have a secret admirer."

"Then who sent this beautiful rose?"

My chair creaks as I sink into it. "Probably my dad."

"I thought you asked your dad if it was him and he vehemently denied it."

"Yeah, well, of course," I roll my eyes.

Rachel points the rose at me. "Dr. Laurel is a genius, but he can't lie worth a damn. If he said it wasn't him, then it's someone else."

"Like who?" Locked doors and tight security don't deter the annual delivery. Last year I even checked the delivery records and the security cameras in the lobby. Nothing. Whoever left the rose snuck in and out of the building like a ghost.

She flashes her eyebrows. "Adam Archer."

"No." I pretend to organize a pile of papers on my desk, but my cheeks are two Bunsen burners.

"He wants in your pants," she singsongs, switching seamlessly from Rachel The Very Professional Executive Assistant to Rachel The Teasing Matchmaking Friend.

"Adam Archer does not want me like that," I wave a hand. "Adam is..." I shake my head. "He's just an old friend. The only thing he's interested in is the business merger. That's the only reason we've been spending more time together lately."

"Friends don't look at friends like he looks at you."

"He's like an older brother." A smoking hot, unrelated, older brother—but seriously, it's not like that. "He's known me since I was a girl. He doesn't like me. Not that way." I push back a stray lock of my hair.

Rachel scoffs. "I'm pretty sure he does. He's asked you out several times."

"Those are working lunches."

"And dinners. He also took you to the aquarium. And the symphony."

"That was a good opportunity to network. Some of the board was there, too."

She narrows her eyes. "Would it be so terrible if he was into you? He's pretty hot. New Olympus' Most Eligible Bachelor like five years in a row. Plus he's heir to the Archer fortune."

"I just…well, he's *him*. And I'm…" My hands flutter helplessly. "I'm me."

"And you're fabulous."

I roll my eyes. "I'm a good researcher. Not so great at anything else."

"Not true," Rachel says gently. "I know you're inexperienced when it comes to men."

"Understatement of the year," I snort. "I've never been on a date." Never even been kissed.

"You've never *realized* you've been on a date," she corrects. "There's a difference. Because I'm pretty sure all these outings with Adam count as dates. He's just such a gentleman, he's taking it slow."

"Do you really think he's…into me?" *Into me?* Do they even say that any more? Kill me now, I sound like a teenager. Which, okay, socially, I am. But really, I can't even wrap my head around what she's suggesting. I spent all my early teens *studying*, not partying. I got into college early and threw myself into a research path as soon as humanly possible, following in the footsteps of my brilliant father.

"Why don't you meet with him tonight and ask him? He wanted to know if you were coming. He had his office call."

I flush even hotter and shuffle some papers on my desk. "He probably wants to discuss the merger."

"Maybe he does. Or maybe he's interested in 'merging' in more ways than one." She hops off the desk and shimmies her hips, singing, "bow chicka wow wow."

"La la la, I can't hear you." I laugh, covering my ears. Then I close my eyes as she continues grinding. "Or see you."

She smacks me on the shoulder and I drop my hands. "You know you love me."

I roll my eyes. She's right, though, I do. Even when she's Rachel The Tease. "I don't have time to date."

"Okay, okay." She holds up her hands. "I'm just saying. You'll have friends there. I know you don't realize it, but you have people who care about you. You don't have to do this all alone."

I nod and plaster on a smile. I appreciate the sentiment. I really do. But she doesn't know what it was like growing up the way I did. My life has never been normal and I accepted it a long time ago.

"That reminds me," Rachel goes to the mini fridge and starts rummaging. "Your father sent something for your costume." She wrinkles her nose and pulls out a crown of glossy dark green leaves. "What is this?"

"A laurel wreath." I smile. "Dad usually wears it. Laurel leaves for Dr. Laurel—get it?"

"No, I would never have gotten that," she deadpans.

I laugh at her sarcasm. "I guess he wants me to wear it for him. And it's a quarter to four which means I have three hours to get ready." I scrub at my aching eyes. "This is going to take a miracle."

"Fortunately, you have me. Today, I'm your fairy godmother. And we have no time to lose." She claps her hands. "You shower. I'll make you tea. Don't bother drying your hair. The stylist will be here in twenty minutes. When he's done, I'll do your makeup."

"Sounds good." I yawn.

"Oh don't do that, you'll make me tired, too. Now, you told me you already got a costume to wear?"

"Yes! I had a dress custom made." I walk to my small closet at the back of my office and open the cabinet with a flourish.

Rachel's mouth drops open. "What. The. Hell. Is. *That?*"

TWO

Beast

I SIP from my champagne glass and narrow my eyes at the ballroom before me.

The bubbles explode on my tongue and I want to spit the liquid out on the floor at the glittering high heels of a passing socialite. She glides by, joining a group of others just like her: beautiful people dressed in expensive finery.

I used to think these people were merely vapid and useless. Now I know the truth. No one who can afford to be in this fucking room is blameless. The rich and powerful became that way by stepping on the necks of the less fortunate.

The place is huge—a cavernous ballroom laid out under several story high columns. The room is full with a vast and glimmering sea of people, each new face more beautiful and powerful than the last.

Once, I bought into it. Less than a decade ago, I came to

a function a lot like this, so full of a young man's idealism. My whole life ahead of me.

All those dreams are bitter ash in my mouth now.

Who I was doesn't matter anymore.

Only who I am now.

Tonight, I begin. I will re-balance the scales of justice. I guard the entrance to the ball, still as a gargoyle. No one looks my way as I study them through the eye holes in my mask.

Everyone's wearing masks tonight. The rich and famous pretend to be gods, their hypocrisy and arrogance never more fully on display. And I'll beat them at their own game. I won't lie or cheat or try to manipulate.

I'll be exactly what I am.

The monster they made me.

A trio of women dressed as Muses openly stare at me. I glare in their direction; they turn away, their laughter giddy as champagne bubbles. An insipid chorus, the perfect soundtrack for this awful event.

Then I see *her*. Dr. Laurel's brilliant daughter.

She's more beautiful than ever. Her skin is so radiant and flushed with youth. Even from across the room, her eyes sparkle. She's full of life and mine have never been more of a mockery than in this moment.

My hands ball into fists even as I wonder:

Did she like my rose?

THREE

Daphne

EVERY YEAR, the rich and famous of New Olympus gather at the Parthenon for the Autumn Gala. Every year—but one—I've dressed up like a princess and floated up the red carpet on my father's arm, only to spend the night lurking next to the wall. The perpetual wallflower.

The spacious ballroom is full with a vast and glimmering sea of people, each new face more beautiful and powerful than the last.

My stomach roils. Should've eaten more. I lean against a gigantic column bathed in green light, doing my best impersonation of a wallflower. *Just part of the scenery.*

"Quite a sight, aren't they?" a smooth voice murmurs in my ear. I nearly leap out of my skin, whirling to face the suave-looking gentleman who emerges from the shadows. His face is handsome, striking, with warm, tan skin and dark brows. His mask is no more than a thin black ribbon, the perfect setting for his black eyes.

"W-what?" I stutter.

"The constellations." Without looking away, he sweeps a hand at the ceiling. I look up and my mouth drops open. The entire ceiling is swathed in dark blue fabric dotted with tiny lights meant to resemble stars. "A clever use of fairy lights."

He studies the ceiling, his profile limned in shadow. He's prettier than I am. Most of the men here are.

I steady myself. I belong here, just the same as him. Even if I don't feel like it. "It's beautiful."

"Worth the thousand dollar ticket?" He raises a brow.

I narrow my eyes. "I know you." The name flashes in my memory. "Armand!" I've met the flashy spa magnate several times at galas like these. He's close friends with the Ubelis. Stylish, charming, and usually up to mischief of some sort or other if the rumors can be believed.

"The one and only." He bows.

"You haven't changed a bit," I blurt, then wince, wishing I could control my mouth. But he only laughs.

"Thank you, darling. You know how to flatter a guy."

"It's true." He looks the same as he always has, other than a touch of grey at his temples. "Not everyone can pull off a jacket like that."

"Shall I return the favor? Not everyone can pull off a... shall we call it a dress? like that. Now who or what are you supposed to be?" He pulls out a monocle and peers through it, studying me like a strange bug under a magnifying glass. "Green fabric with brown at the edges. And is that...bark on your bodice?"

I stifle a groan. "I'm Daphne of the myth. She turned into a laurel tree."

"Hmm," Armand murmurs.

"I was trying to be clever," I mumble.

Two beautiful women traipse past us, one blonde, one brunette. Both dressed in togas that hug their butts and plunge between their breasts. Sexy Aphrodite and Slutty Athena. The blonde flutters her fingers at Armand. He smiles but gives a small shake of his head, and she turns away with a pout.

Rachel was right. Dressing like a tree was a mistake. I hold my chin up, pretending I don't care.

"You are clever, darling." Unbelievably, Armand turns back to me. I wrack my brain for what I know about him. Owner of a chain of spas, a top fashion line, and hair and skin treatment products shipped all over the world. "I would expect nothing less from you...Dr. Laurel." He tweaks my leafy crown of laurels.

"Oh, call me Daphne. Dr. Laurel is my father."

"Daphne." He inclines his head. "How *is* your father?"

"Much better, thank you," I repeat the company line. His stroke is common knowledge, widely reported, much to the board's dismay.

"And you, the youngest CEO in New Olympus." Armand is back to studying me with his monocle. "Perhaps ever."

"Not quite. Adam Archer claimed that title when he took over Archer Industries for his father."

"But that was years ago. Now you ascend to the throne. I wonder if Adam will be jealous."

"Not of me." I blush.

"Mmmm," Armand purrs, tucking the monocle away. "I think you underestimate yourself."

"I don't think so."

"You're here, aren't you? Young, beautiful, successful."

"Acting like a wallflower. Which is fitting, because I'm

dressed as shrubbery." I spread my hands to present my sartorial faux pas.

Armand's laugh lights tingles up and down my spine. I don't mind his flirting—I know I'm not his type—but he certainly is handsome.

"We can't have that, beautiful Daphne. Come." He takes my hand and draws me away from the column. My options are to protest and make a scene, or follow.

I choose to follow. "Where are you taking me?" My stomach rumbles. I put a hand over it, mortified.

Armand pauses. "Perhaps I should get you something from the buffet?"

"Oh no, I couldn't possibly. I'm afraid I'll spill something on myself. I get clumsy when I'm nervous." Then I slam my mouth shut. *Argh, must engage brain before talking!* This is why I shouldn't socialize.

But Armand only chuckles. "Very well." He draws me into his embrace. "Do you dance?"

"Not really." My limbs are wooden.

"Sway with me then." His eyes mesmerize me, and I grow supple in his arms. "That's it."

At one end of the ballroom, a full piece orchestra plays a jazzy version of the Sleeping Beauty waltz. Armand leads me smoothly between the other dancers. My full skirt swishes satisfyingly around Armand's lean legs. Okay, well this isn't too hard.

"We make a perfect pair," he tells me, and I almost believe him. Heads turn as we pass. For a moment I close my eyes and imagine I'm the beauty in the arms of her prince.

"There," Armand murmurs in my ear. "You're not a wallflower anymore. No one can take their eyes off you."

I draw back, my cheeks in full blaze. "Thank you. You're very kind."

He lets me out for a twirl and I follow his lead, giggling.

"You're welcome, my lady. But there's something you should know." He leans in close to whisper, "I am never kind." He pulls back and I get a glimpse of the calculating look in his dark eyes.

Tingles run up and down my spine, but I relax. In the past few months, I've dealt with more deceit and machinations than in my entire lifetime. And that's just dealing with Belladonna's board of directors. All in a day's work for a CEO.

I meet his gaze straight on. "So you're acting for your benefit?"

"Always. But not only mine." He promenades me past a beautiful blonde in a silvery sheath. The Gala sponsor and hostess, the famous Cora Ubeli, standing in a receiving line of guests. Armand cuts through them and jerks his chin at me. I try to restrain my wild blushes. Cora gives me a gracious wave and smile.

"See?" Armand murmurs, twirling me away. "You're the belle of the ball tonight."

"Me?" I laugh. "No way."

"I've heard nothing but rumors about your intelligence, your wit, your beauty."

"Stop it." My cheeks burn even hotter. "I'm just a scientist."

"On the cusp of great discoveries."

"I hope so." I bite my lip. "But no guarantees. Most scientists try their whole life to make one life changing discovery. "

"Is that why you're seeking the merger with Archer Industries?"

I stiffen in his arms. "What do you know about that?"

"Just what the papers report, *bella donna*."

"Don't call me that."

"No? I've always wondered why your father named his company after a poisonous flower?"

"He named it for my mother. Her name was Isabella. And she was beautiful."

"The original Bella Donna. I see." We whirl together for a few more beats before he adds, "She passed her looks to you."

"Thank you." *Must. Stop. Blushing.*

The song ends. We break apart and clap. Now that the room has stopped spinning, I notice the throngs of people staring at us, studying me behind their masks. My own Greek chorus.

I shiver. Armand smooths his hands down my arms as if to soothe me. Up close, I realize there's more to his costume than the monocle and red velvet jacket. A pair of silky wings are folded against his back. Black to match his eyes.

"So, what are you?" I ask, fighting to keep a grip on my calm. "A fallen angel?"

"Hermes, of course." He leans in and kisses my cheek. "I even have a message for you."

"A message?"

"A warning. Tonight you're Daphne, from the myth?"

I nod shakily.

He dips his head close and whispers in my ear. "Beware Apollo."

"Daphne!"

I whirl in the direction of the shout. A crowd of toga wearers parts like a white sea. And there he is, striding towards me, dressed in white from collar to shoes, a crown of golden leaves on his head.

Adam Archer.

He's golden and handsome and I think about all the things Rachel said earlier. About how the outings we've been on were actually *dates*.

"Adam," I greet him, holding out my hands. To my dismay, he brings them to his mouth and kisses my fingers. Does this mean Rachel was *right*? Or is he just being overly chivalrous?

"Daphne. You look so beautiful." His teeth flash, white as his tux. A few feet away, Aphrodite and Athena sigh and strike a pose, their assets on full display. But Adam only looks at me. My heart flutters.

"A-and you look handsome." I free my hands and press fingers to my lips. I worked hard to lose my shy stutter. But all my intelligence flies out the window whenever I'm with Adam. And then I realize the fingers on my lips are the ones he just kissed and my cheeks flame all over again. It's good I barely put any blush on since my cheeks are going to be a perpetual rosy red.

Adam really is the handsomest man in the room. White blond hair, a sculpted profile and body of an Olympic athlete. The gods wept when they made him.

And he's at least the tenth richest man in the room, I hear Rachel's whisper, like a devil on my shoulder.

I turn to introduce Armand, but he's disappeared completely, as if he's flown away. *Just like Hermes.*

If Adam is wondering why I'm looking around, he doesn't show it. "I missed you, darling," he draws me close. My eyes catch on the tiny golden lyre pinned to his lapel. *Beware Apollo.*

I blink and focus on Adam, who's still talking. "I called your office to see if we could ride together."

"Sorry." I'm blushing. The only way my cheeks could

get redder is if I turned inside out. *Breathe. Remember to breathe, dammit.* "I must've been in the lab."

"Poor, sweet Cinderella." He draws me onto the ballroom floor. "Once our companies merge, you won't have to work so hard."

His hands—they're on my *body*. Intimately touching me. Well, more intimately than I'm usually ever touched.

His right hand rests on my waist right above the curve of my hip like he's held me there every day of his life. Even Armand wasn't so bold. Adam's left hand holds my hand in a commanding grip as he guides me across the floor.

"I-I don't mind it." I struggle to get my tongue back in order. "I mean, I like the lab. I like my work."

"I know you do," he soothes. "Your board tells me you barely leave Belladonna's basement."

Wait, what? "They do?" I bristle. *Who's been talking to him behind my back?* "They shouldn't be talking about me to outsiders—"

"But I'm not an outsider, am I, sweet? I've been an ally of Belladonna since the beginning. If my father hadn't wanted me to take over Archer Industries, I'd be in the lab with you, just like in the olden days with your father... speaking of whom, how is Dr. Laurel?"

"He's fine." The rote response pops out of my mouth.

Adam says nothing, just keeps looking at me. And I crumble, sagging in his arms.

"I don't know," I whisper as a fist tightens around my chest. Yes, tonight is weird with both of us in these fancy clothes in this super fancy place, but this is *Adam*. He was one of my father's beloved students. A protege.

So I tell him the truth. "Dad's not getting better. The doctors wanted to start PT weeks ago, but he's still so sick." My voice trembles.

Everywhere I look, members of Olympus society stare at me. Vultures, all of them. Sharks sensing blood in the water.

With a reassuring murmur, Adam guides me to a corner of the room, snagging a glass of champagne from a server's tray.

He offers it to me and I shake my head. I never drink, never partied in college. I'm a lightweight, and I haven't eaten anything.

"I insist," Adam presses the glass to my lips until I take a gulp. "There, that's better. I'll take care of you."

My shoulders soften. Of course he's right. Adam's not an outsider. My father thinks of him as a son. I used to think of him as a brother—

"Sweet Daphne," he brushes a curl out of my face. "All grown up."

I flush from forehead to cleavage. I don't think I can deny any more that Rachel was right. Adam doesn't think of me as a little sister, not anymore.

"Don't worry about the merger. Or the board. I can handle them."

I draw in a breath. "Thank you, Adam. But I'm CEO now. I should—"

"I'm more than happy to take on all duties as CEO, so you can spend all your time in the lab. If you choose to live there, that's fine. As long as your nights belong to me." He winks.

I stare at his beautiful features. The room behind him is swimming, a blur of color.

"Nights?" I squeak. "You want me to...work with you? At night?"

He chuckles, tilting his head. He's looking at me like I'm adorable. Adorable and naive. "I think we'd work well together."

"Like, business partners?"

"Business partners. And more." His hand settles into the small of my back, pressing me close. *Oh.* I might be a virgin, but I aced my anatomy classes. And Adam is perfectly formed—in all areas.

"Don't tell me you don't want this," he murmurs in my ear.

"I...don't *not* want it." Way to commit, Daphne!

Rachel was right. Adam is into me. So much he'd like to be *inside* me if the hardness against my stomach is any indication. "I don't know what to say. I thought you just wanted Belladonna."

"I do want Belladonna. The merger makes sense. But so do we."

I swallow. Adam is looking at me expectantly, a half smile on his breathtaking face. Any other woman would swoon if she was in my shoes. *So why don't I feel happy?* "What about my father?"

"What about him?" Adam tilts his head, casting half his perfect profile into shadow.

"He's fragile right now. Won't this be a shock?"

"We can wait, if you like. Until your father is better."

"I-I'd like that. There's just so much going on." I step away, rubbing my temples. "The board, the merger. The press keeps hinting that Belladonna is on the brink of bankruptcy." *And they may be right.*

"Why don't you let me worry about all that?"

Because I'm a big girl. I don't need a man to save me. The retort is on my tongue when the band strikes up a rousing Strauss waltz. The room swirls with dancing couples. The figures start to blur...

I touch my face, wishing I had my glasses. It's silly,

but whenever I'm stuck on a problem, I switch from contacts to glasses or vice versa. A literal new way of seeing things.

"A-Adam?"

"Yes, sweet?"

"I think I need a moment. My contacts don't seem to be working right." *There are two of you.*

"All right, Daphne. I'll wait." He ushers me out of the ballroom, past a duo of hulking security guards to a private hall.

I pause with my hand on the bathroom door. "I won't be long."

"Good girl," Adam says, already turning away and pulling his cellphone from his pocket. Even doing something as mundane as checking his texts, he looks like a model.

I turn away, making a face. Adam's always been a little overbearing but tonight he's coming on strong. I need an ally. I wish Rachel was here.

The bathroom is empty and blissfully quiet. I linger a few extra moments in the dark stall before emerging to wash my hands in the marble sink. My head throbs. My hands blur.

I knew I shouldn't have worn these contacts. So what if my glasses make me look like a nerd? I am one.

Gritting my teeth, I remove the offending lenses. *There, that's better.* Now if the room would just stop spinning.

"Daphne?"

I whirl with a yelp. Armand stands in the doorway between the bathroom and the ladies parlor. I didn't even hear him come in.

"What are you doing here?" Without my contacts, his far away features are a bit blurry, but he stands out, a dark specter in the midst of pink and white marble. "This is the ladies room!"

"And I'm the biggest queen here." He strikes a pose. "At least until Philip Waters arrives. Are you feeling all right? Your pupils are dilated."

"I'm...fine," I slur, leaning back on the counter. "Drink hit me the wrong way."

"Hmmm." He comes closer, leaning in to study me. "You haven't been imbibing belladonna, have you?"

"What?"

"Renaissance women took belladonna to make their pupils larger—"

"I know that," I flap my hand. "Believe me, I know everything about belladonna the plant that there is to know. And I have not imbibed it." I'm just feeling a wee bit queasy...

"Good. Because you're late for a very important date."

"With Adam?"

"Not him, you sly girl. You've got another secret admirer. A beast of a man."

"What?"

"I was told to give you this." Armand hands me a rose.

I hold it close, staring at the whorl of red petals. "Who sent this?" The rose is exactly like the one left in my office. *Rosa x hybrida.* I know roses—my mother made sure of that.

It can't be a coincidence. I'm this close to knowing who my secret admirer is.

"I don't know. Big man in a scary mask. But what I wouldn't give to find out." He waggles his brows.

I put a hand to my head. Is this really happening?

"He wants you to meet him in the labyrinth. Take all right turns. Oh, and he says the future of Belladonna depends on it."

What?

There's a knock on the door in the outer parlor. "Daphne?" comes Adam's muffled voice.

I stiffen, clutching the rose close. Is it a bad sign that I'm so tempted to grab this lifeline Armand is offering me—or the fact that it feels like a lifeline in the first place? What's wrong with me? Any woman here would kill to be in my place with Adam waiting on the other side of that door for her.

"Is that Adam Archer?" Armand asks. "The plot thickens."

"He's worried about me." I bite my lip.

"You do look flushed. Are you sure you're all right?"

I shake my head and hold up the mysterious rose. "Help me?"

"This way." Armand grabs my hand, guiding me down the line of stalls, as if helping me sneak out of the ladies bathroom is the most normal thing in the world.

At the end of the bathroom is a giant gilt mirror. Armand pushes a hidden button and I gasp when it swings open a crack, revealing a tiny door.

"Never come to a party without a planned escape route," Armand announces, pulling a key out of his jacket pocket and fitting it to the door's lock.

"Seriously?" I gape.

"It's New Olympus." He shrugs. "Nothing is as it seems."

"Thanks, Hermes," I giggle. Tomorrow I'll think this is all a weird dream. But right now, the champagne is really hitting me.

"Daphne?" Adam's voice echoes, getting closer. "Are you in here?"

I should run to him. But instead, I squeeze behind the mirror, frantic to get away. "Cover me," I mouth to Armand.

Through the looking glass I go.

Armand nods and closes the door behind me.

I step into some sort of low ceilinged hallway. It's completely dark but I can feel around with my hands and I trust Armand not to send me towards a dead end. But this night is getting stranger by the second. I stumble on, feeling my way with my hands and find another door, this one unlocked.

It swings open and I emerge into the night air.

FOUR

Daphne

IT'S COOL OUTSIDE, and gods it feels good. Strains of music float above my head. I'm at the foot of a large staircase, the twin to the one I entered at the front of the Parthenon. This one leads to a balcony where guests can gather. Unlike inside, there are no stars in this sky. But a path of tiny twinkling lights leads to my destination.

The labyrinth.

The maze is made of towering hedges, shaped into thick walls of dark green. But at least the elaborate decorations mean that standing light sconces are set up every five feet or so, so I can see in spite of the dark, moonless night. Evening mist floats along the ground.

Creepy much? I shiver and wrap my arms around the soft bark of my costume's waist.

I look down at the rose clutched in my hand. I held it so hard in the darkness, the thorns pricked my hand and there are two dots of blood on my palm. I wipe them against the dark bark of my bodice. So much for not getting anything on my dress. I glance down the labyrinth.

The future of Belladonna depends on it. What does that mean? Our precarious position isn't a secret. My father is ill, leaving me at the helm. Even with the Ubeli Foundation's generous donations, Belladonna is sucking through money. The possible merger with Archer Industries is a lifeline.

This invitation is probably a prank. Armand or Adam or someone is playing a joke.

But if it's one of them, then that means they know the secret of the rose. *My secret admirer.*

I clutch the rose like a talisman and blunder forward, entering the labyrinth. Immediately, the noise and music of the party becomes muted. A shiver creeps its way up my spine at the sudden quiet.

The box hedges stand about two feet above my head on both sides and up ahead the path forks left and right. Which way to go? Then I remember what Armand said. Keep turning *right*. That's easy enough to remember.

But then another shiver runs through me as I look around and stumble a little. Dang, I really should have eaten something. I blink a few times, trying to think. I giggle. Usually it's not this hard to think. But then I frown and *try* hard.

Because what if it isn't Armand or Adam? Sure Armand gave me the rose but is he really the most trustworthy? It's not like I know the guy, not really. Am I really just going to wander blindly out into the dark to meet some stranger dangling my company's survival out in front of my nose?

If this was a horror movie, I'd *definitely* be the first to die. Dumb girl walking out into the dark alone. Then again, I'm a virgin. Don't they kill the virgins last?

I clap a hand over my mouth to keep in another hysterical giggle. Dear gods, I should just go back to the party. I stop in my tracks and look over my shoulder.

But the harder I listen, the more I actually *can* hear voices and the occasional laugh somewhere around me, probably others also exploring the labyrinth.

I scrub a hand down my face. This is not a freaking horror movie. I'm just being silly and letting myself get freaked out. There are people around everywhere and the security at a party like this has to be insane.

No one would try anything while we were in a public place and literally all I'd have to do is scream. I mean, the party is being thrown by Cora Ubeli and her husband was supposed to be a big bad mob boss—and that's not even taking into account the rumors about Mrs. Ubeli herself.

No one's dumb enough to try to screw with any of the Ubeli's guests.

I blink hard to reorient myself, then turn right at the fork and head further into the labyrinth. Chill bumps race down my arms, both from the cold night air and the dark night. And I do really *want* to know who's been sending the roses all these years. It's never felt like someone malicious.

Strings of lights are woven into the hedges here and there, along with the occasional standing sconce, but it's only barely enough to see where I'm going.

So pretty. I sigh and trace my fingertips along the lights.

Pretty lights in the dark night. Haha! I trip again.

Whoops! I barely catch myself and frown down at the mist covering the ground.

Well, that's why I'm tripping. I can barely see my feet. Ooh look, another fork in the path. Another right turn. More twinkly lights.

But the lights seem to blink in and out, and for a second I can't make out anything at all. The mist is especially heavy here for some reason, like someone's blown a fog machine over the garden.

"Hello?" I call out, waving a hand uselessly at the mist to try to see.

I blink hard and take another step down the path. My step stumbles though and the path spins crazily.

Whoa, I don't feel so good. I blink again and reach out for balance. My hand brushes against shrubbery but I can't get a good grip and stumble again.

Shit. When was the last time I ate? I have a bad habit of working through meals and today I don't think I even grabbed anything from the snack machines, I was so anxious about the newest round of experiments.

And then there was the champagne... The world slants sideways for a moment, mists and hedges and ground all becoming distorted in front of me like a funhouse mirror.

What the—?

I stumble forward and finally make it all the way down the path.

It's a dead end.

There's no one waiting for me.

I frown and grab my dizzy head. Is this all some joke? Someone's funny idea of screwing with me? Or did I take a wrong turn and not realize it? I'm *really* not feeling so good.

I hold a hand out to the sculpted branches of the box hedge for balance. I really need to get back to the party. Have to— Have to eat something before I pass out.

I turn around to head back—

And scream.

In front of me, blocking the path back into the rest of the maze, is a monster. Huge. Horns sticking out of his head. A freaking demon monster! Heading through the mists towards me.

I scream and stumble backwards into the hedge. Dark-leafed branches scratch at me.

"You're hallucinating," I whisper frantically to myself. "Someone spiked the punch." I've heard of that happening before. People spiking punch with party drugs so that parties turn into, like, orgies. And whatever they put in this time is hitting me way, *way* wrong.

The scary demon monster takes another step towards me.

I whimper, blinking over and over as it comes in and out of focus, swathed in mist.

Not real. He *isn't* real.

But he sure as hell looks real, all six massive feet of him. Chest like a champion wrestler with huge, oversized muscles, barely constrained by a dress shirt, no jacket.

As he comes closer, dark eyes glare down at me from a bronzed demon face. He's a— A monster.

"What do you want from me?" I whisper, fear cinching my chest tight. I should scream. I need to scream people so can come help me. But my vocal cords are frozen like my legs.

He grins and I frown. Wait, his mouth, it's different. I blink repeatedly. Is he— Is he wearing a *mask?*

"What do I want from you?" His voice is a low, brutal growl. "Everything, little girl."

Oh shit. Run. I need to *run*.

But he's backed me into a corner. There's nowhere to go where he won't catch me.

"I'm going to take everything from you and—" he growled.

But I never hear the end of his threat because right then, I pass the fuck out.

FIVE

Daphne

I BLINK my eyes blearily and lift a hand to my head. What the— That was the craziest dream. I scrub my hand down my face and sit up.

And then shriek, because where the hell am I?

I jump out of the fancy four poster bed—a bed that *isn't* mine—and my feet hit a cold stone floor. The whole room's made of stone. There's a giant empty fireplace with a snarling beast head. It reminds me of the creature the night before.

Shit. Shit shit shit. This is *bad*. I blink hard and shake my pounding head. I have a headache from hell. Was I *drugged*? Oh my gods, I was drugged and then *kidnapped*. I'm not wearing my tree costume, just the nude-colored camisole and slip I was wearing underneath. Holy shit. Holy shit.

I run to the window. The glass is old, thickened at the edges. The stone sill is freezing to touch. Outside is a several-story drop down a worn stone face to a lawn below. Mist swirls over the trimmed grass and hedges, obscuring the road and the forest beyond. Not that I can see much far off detail without my contact lenses.

I swing back and look around the room again. Weapon. I need a weapon. Shit! In all those years of schooling I took, how did I never take a self-defense class? There's a lamp in the corner that looks heavy.

But right as I head towards it, the huge wooden door opens. I clap a hand over my mouth to hold in a shriek when a man—oh gods, the same one from last night, bits and pieces are starting to come back—comes into the room.

"You're awake," he says in his low baritone. Even without my glasses, I see the truth. He's wearing a mask. Not the same as last night. There aren't horns this time—maybe that was part of the drugged hallucinations?

This mask is smooth and covers only the left half of his face, including most of his nose. I'm too distracted by the mask and, ya know, the fact that I've been kidnapped by a most likely psycho killer to pay too much attention to the other half of his face, other than to note that he's young, maybe in his thirties.

I scramble backwards up against the windowsill. "Please don't hurt me," I whisper, my heart pounding a thousand miles a minute.

"You're not safe," he says, standing still as stone in the doorway. "Someone tried to drug you."

I'm frozen as well, only able to stare at him. Uh, duh, someone not only tried to drug me, they did—*Him*. Before he brought me back to his creepy lair.

"Please let me go."

"Not until I'm sure you're safe. Who would've drugged you?"

Is he serious right now? "No one that I know."

He shakes his head, a bitter smile curving his lips. "You don't see them for what they are."

"You're the one wearing a mask."

He takes a step into the room and I flatten myself back against the window even though I know it's useless as he stalks closer. His foot falls in time with my heartbeat: boom. Boom. Boom.

"In New Olympus, evil doesn't have to wear a mask. It parades around, looking beautiful, for all to see. But underneath it's rotten to the core."

"I don't know what you're talking about." I touch my face, frowning when I don't feel my glasses there. "Please just let me go."

"What? Didn't you like your rose? Your mother did so love them."

He pulls his hand from behind his back and produces a perfect red rose. I can smell it from here. It's the same hybrid from last night. And the one on my desk. And every year since I was eighteen...

"You?" I gasp. "Who *are* you?"

He takes another step closer and runs the blush of the rose petals down my cheek. My first instinct is to jerk back but instead I straighten my spine and look him in the eye. He drags the silken petals down the side of my cheek, along my throat and down along my exposed collarbones. It raises involuntary goosebumps but I don't look away.

I'm not going to cower from this man, no matter the fact that I'm scared out of my pants. If only I were wearing pants. I'm suddenly very aware of just how little I'm wearing.

His eyes are a dark, stormy chocolate. And gods, does he have to be so large? The huge span of his chest blocks out almost my entire vision. I've never been so near anyone so... masculine. I ought to be terrified, and I am, don't get me wrong. But I'm not going to cower in fear in front of him.

"The question is, Dr. Daphne Laurel, who are *you*? Are you as corrupt as the rest of them?"

I frown. "Corrupt? I don't underst—"

"Stop playing innocent," he suddenly booms, grabbing my upper arm in an unrelenting grip.

I shriek and he lets go but his eyes are thunderous as he looms over me. "You will be tested. Are you an innocent girl just trying to find the cure for the disease that took her mother's life? Or are you a money-grubbing business executive like your father?"

"What are you talking about? My father isn't—"

"Your father," he practically spits, "talked a good game. But as soon as he could, he traded his ideals for a fortune. I guess making money from beauty creams is better than trying to cure the incurable?"

"It's not incurable!" I shout, shoving at his chest. "We're close. And who the hell are you to judge me? Belladonna had to diversify or we wouldn't have had enough money to continue our research. The research that will save lives one day!"

He grabs both of my wrists, easily subduing me. "So passionate for your cause," he smirks. "Or like daddy, lying is just second nature to you by this point."

"Let go of me, you son of a bitch." I yank to get away from him but it's like trying to wrestle a bear. He's too strong and his grip is like iron. But he doesn't do anything other than hold my wrist in the shackle of his hands. He just stands there patiently until I finally stop struggling. Furious, I huff hair out of my face and glare at him.

"I know I can't trust a word from your pretty mouth.

But that's all right. Ever since you dropped into my lap last night, I've been thinking. I *was* going to just destroy your father's company and revel in watching it burn. But then..." He pauses and frowns. "Then there's you."

What does that mean? I feel my mouth drop open slightly. This entire thing is insane. This *man* is obviously insane.

"Who *are* you? What did we ever do to you?"

"All that matters is what you choose to do now. I'm going to give you a chance to save your company, little girl. It's the only offer you're going to get, so pay attention."

"You don't have any power over—"

"But I do. I own the future of Belladonna, in point of fact."

I laugh. But then I sober. Maybe I should just play along with the delusional man. If I play along, will he actually let me go?

But he sees right through me. "You don't believe me." He smiles and leans in. "Go ask Daddy dearest. Ask him how he got out of debt six years ago when the company was in trouble. Then again, I doubt he'll tell you the truth so I'll save you the trouble. He sold all his patents. To *me.*"

"No," I laugh. "He would never do that."

But the man in front of me isn't laughing.

I just keep shaking my head. "You don't know what you're talking about. What patents?"

"All of them, Daphne. Every bit of research, every right to bring your findings to market—it all belongs to me."

"You're lying," I whisper. Dad would never, *ever,* sell the patents. We'd have no company without them. Our research wouldn't be *our* research anymore. "Dad would never..."

"He thought it was temporary. That he'd be able to buy

them back when times were better. I leased them back to Belladonna for a time. But time's run out." He smirks. "Belladonna owns nothing. Your father can't worm his way out of his mistakes this time. It's time for his sins to finally catch up with him."

"Why are you so hateful?" I jerk back from him and he finally lets go of my wrists. "You're a monster!"

He tilts his head at me, the black half-mask making his face blank and creepy as hell. "Maybe. I am what they made me. The question is, what have they made you?"

"*They* haven't made me anything. I'm my own woman."

"We'll see. We'll see, Daphne." The way he says my name...it's so familiar, like he knows me, not like we're strangers that just met in the worst of circumstances. Gods, how long has he been stalking me? How long has he been fantasizing this non-existent relationship between us? The roses have been coming for years and years. Has it really been him this whole time? And why is he so fixated on my family?

"I've decided I want to give you a chance, Daphne. I want you to submit to me, let me break you down, crack you open, and see your truths. This is the only way I'll consider saving Belladonna."

"You're crazy," I choke out.

"I'm *merciful*." His jaw hardens. "Something your father knows nothing about. But I won't force anything on you. I'll even let you take a day to think about it." He walks back to the door, and to my shock, opens it wide.

I start to hurry towards it but before I can run through it, he grabs my arm. "But rest assured, if you aren't back tomorrow by sunset, I'll move forward with my plans to bring Belladonna to its knees and then break open the bottle of Chateau Margaux I've been saving while I scatter the ashes."

Our eyes lock and I search his eyes, looking for madness, looking for some indication that this entire thing is some sort of fever dream. But all I see is...warmth? Like he's hoping for something? And determination. He'll follow through on his threat.

I'm so confused. None of this makes any sense.

"There's a taxi waiting out front. He'll take you wherever you need to go."

Then he releases my arm and I flee out the room, down the hall and down the elegant central stairway and out the front door.

I STUMBLE out into the sunshine, looking back over my shoulder as I go, sure it's some twisted trick. He's going to drag me back any second, laughing at my foolishness believing he'd ever let me go.

But no, he remains a dark, forbidding shadow in the doorway. I'm not going to take another moment second-guessing my good-fortune. I turn and this time I don't look back. I sprint towards the taxi, yank open the back door, and slam it behind me.

"Drive!" I shout at the elderly cabbie.

"Where, miss?"

"Anywhere! Just get me out of here."

He puts the car in gear and we pull forward on the circular drive that surrounds an elaborate fountain. Only when we're almost out of the driveway do I look back. What the hell *is* this place?

It's a legit castle. Gray-green stone, towers, turrets, even battlements. The towering structure is built on a hill, surrounded by a maze of hedges and green lawn. The further down the curving drive we go, the more gardens come into view. One of the side sections is full of blooming flowers that look like roses. But beyond it is a towering hedge, almost like the labyrinth.

I remember last night and shudder.

The car turns onto the main road, rolling past giant, forbidding iron gates. I turn back around in my seat and drag my hands down my face. What the hell just happened? That man was insane. Nothing he said was true.

"So where to now, miss?" the cabbie looks at me in the rearview. He has old, slightly rheumy eyes that I bet have seen a lot.

"To the nearest p—" I bite my lip and squeeze my eyes shut. *Police station*. I need him to take me to the nearest police station. Right?

But...

What if?

What if there was even the tiniest bit of truth to what the Beast back there said? If Dad really *did* sell the patents? I grab my stomach. Gods, I feel sick.

Yeah, because that crazy bastard drugged you! Which is why you need to go directly to the police station, do not pass go, do not collect a hundred dollars, no questions!

But there's something Dad hasn't been telling me. He's been bad ever since the stroke, but it's something more. He's gotten closed off. He pretends to be asleep when I stop by so he won't have to talk to me. He thinks I don't know, but I do. I thought he just didn't like looking weak in front of me but what if...

"Lady, you gotta give me a destination or we're just

gonna keep driving in circles. I mean, I'm on a meter so it's fine with me but—"

"New Olympus city. Belladonna research labs." I sit up straighter. If I go to Dad first, I won't get a straight answer. No matter how much I've done for the company, he still sees me as his little girl. I need to find out the truth, no matter how much it hurts.

THREE HOURS LATER, I step out of a ride share at my father's townhouse, clutching a stack of papers to my chest. I spent the last few hours scouring my Dad's offices at Belladonna, hoping against hope that I'd find evidence to refute what the Beast who stole me claimed this morning.

Instead... I swallow hard against the lump in my throat. *No, don't even think it.* Dad will be able to explain. He'll tell me how this is all some misunderstanding. A mistake in paperwork that the Beast is exploiting somehow. Making it out to be something it's not.

Dad wouldn't...*couldn't* betray everything we've worked for like this.

Dad's nurse Gemma opens the door and a smile lights her face. "Oh Daphne darling, your daddy will be so happy to see you. I know he wants to hear all about how the ball went last night. And that handsome fella Adam Archer. Rumor has it the two of you are getting hot and heavy."

What? The ball feels about a million years ago but I smooth my expression and put on what I hope is a polite smile. "Is my father awake? I really need to talk to him."

"Aw honey, what's wrong? You look like you had yourself a piece of porcupine pie for breakfast."

Gemma's almost as old as Dad and has been working as

a nurse for decades. Usually I like her spunky colloquialisms and interest in all the town gossip, but not today. I'm on a mission.

"Sorry, Gem, I really need to see Dad."

She frowns but steps back from the door to let me through. "Okay, baby, come on in. He just woke up from a nap and I know seeing you will brighten his day."

Ha, I think. Not likely.

I pass the living room and the bay window where someone, probably Gemma, has propped a painting of Thornhill's gardens. The view is exactly what I used to see when I looked out the window of my mother's home.

Mom and I used to curl up with pillows and blankets and read fairytales when it was raining outside. Everything always seemed extra magical when it was raining, like wizards and fairy godmothers were more likely to pop out of the woods when mist covered the earth after a good rainstorm. My chest aches the way it always does when I think of Mom.

When we lost her, I had no one to talk to. Dad was so lost in grief, and the only person I ever could really talk to about her left not long after she died.

Gods, I haven't thought about Logan in such a long time. He and Adam were my dad's research assistants back in the day.

Adam always seemed...unreachable, unattainable. He was surrounded by co-eds, the golden boy everyone wanted a piece of. But Logan was quiet, studious. He went to college on scholarship and was devoted to his studies. A lot like me.

So we'd study together and during late night study sessions and sometimes in the lab, we'd get to talking. I was only nineteen and he was twenty-eight but science is a universal language. And he knew about Mom and everything we were trying to do to save her.

I wish I could talk to him now. He'd know how to make sense out of this. Dad always treated me like a little kid but Logan treated me like an equal. I was hurt when he suddenly left without saying goodbye, but apparently he got a really good post doc across the country and had to leave right away.

People leave and let you down. Seems like a lesson I should have learned a lot earlier than now but I guess I've been stubborn to the end. I turn away from the bay window and push up the stairs. I'm not a child anymore.

Finally I'm at Dad's door and I pause. My heart is racing. Gods, what am I doing here? Because in spite of the many times people have disappointed me in my life, Dad never has. And there could be other explanations...right? I mean, okay, there are some unexplained blanks in the accounting records. But Dad was never good with that kind of stuff.

He's a lab guy like me. He might be just as clueless about all this. Yes, I know he's the CEO, but that doesn't mean someone didn't take advantage of an old man... I should've taken a closer interest in the company as a whole long before his stroke. Gods, how could I have just let him shoulder the entire burden? What kind of daughter does that?

But I'm here now and we'll figure this out together. Whatever *this* is. Whoever is trying to screw with our company. I take a deep breath and then push through the door.

Dad's reading a thick tome, but he looks up at my entrance and his face immediately brightens. His once salt and pepper hair is now all white and I'll still never get used to seeing him in the hospital bed we had installed up in his room, machines constantly monitoring his vitals.

"Daphne." He sets the book aside. "I wasn't expecting you today. To what do I owe this pleasure?"

"Dad, there's a problem." I rush to his bedside, trying to ignore how unsettling it is to see the changes in him. "Someone's been stealing from the company. Or something. I don't know how to explain what I'm seeing. But I need your help to figure it out or else we're in trouble."

I start to spread the papers out on his bed but when I next glance up at Dad's face, it's gone ashen.

"Dad?" My hands start to tremble. He doesn't look surprised. He doesn't look surprised at all by what I'm showing him.

"You knew?"

He doesn't say anything. He just looks down at his lap.

My throat closes up. No. No no no. "Dad, tell me these are just accounting errors. It can't be true. You didn't... I mean, you didn't really *sell* the patents."

"Who told you that?" His head jerks up and there's an expression on his face I've never seen before. He looks manic and angry and afraid all at the same time.

"Dad!" my voice breaks. "What's going on? Please. You have to tell me."

My father's hand shoots out and clamps around my wrist. "Leave it alone, Daph. Walk away. Walk away now."

My mouth drops open in shock. Is he serious? "This is our company, everything we've worked for."

But his hands are shaking. "He's too strong." His cheeks had color when I came in but they've gone completely pale.

"Who?" I cry. "Who, Daddy? Who did you sell to? Who's doing this to us?" I've never seen my father like this before. I was expecting him to tell me this was all nonsense.

An accounting error, or that he'd never seen this before and we'd track down the culprit together.

But this? He knows my tormentor. Oh gods, how long has this been going on?

"Tell me everything," I demand.

But he shakes his head vehemently. "This will never touch you."

Oh Daddy, if you only knew. "What does he want? Tell me that at least if you won't tell me who it is."

A tear crests my father's eye and rolls down his cheek. "I'm so sorry, bella mia. This is all my fault. I hope that he'll consider my death payment enough." He coughs a long, raking cough. "I don't think it will be long now."

"Dad," I cry, reaching down and hugging his skin-and-bones body. Gods, when did he get so skinny? "Don't say that! Never say that. What are you talking about? We can fight this." I let him go only when another coughing fit hits.

Why didn't Gemma tell me it was getting this bad? But one look at my Dad and I know why. He told her not to. My stubborn ass of a father. Always thinking he can carry things on his own. Always treating me as if I'm a little child, even though I've spent my whole life hurrying to grow up faster so I could share the burden *with* him.

And now he's just given up. He's not even fighting. He'll never get better if he doesn't even *try*. He had a stroke but plenty of people come back from that and live fulfilling lives. But this... I look down at his emaciated body.

Does he have pneumonia? And what the hell has Gemma been doing about it? We've kept her on because she gets on well with Dad but if she's not giving him the care he needs, I don't care if we need to get Nurse Ratched in here.

I grab Dad by his cheeks and force him to look me in the eye. "You are *not* giving up. You are going to *fight*, do you hear me? I don't care about the company." That's a lie, but right now, all Dad needs to focus on is getting better. I repeat it out loud: "You just need to focus on getting better. That's all that matters right now."

I bite my bottom lip and then I do something I've never done before. I lie to my father. "And to ensure you can do that, I'll do as you ask. I'll go away. I'll take an extended vacation so you know I'm safe, okay?"

All the tension leaves Dad's body and he sinks back into the pillows. "Oh thank the gods. Yes, baby, get as far away from here as you can."

I nod. "Okay, Dad. I will." I lean over and give him another hug. "You just focus on getting better."

I stand on the sidewalk outside of his apartment. The weather's turned cold, but I welcome the numbing feeling.

I make a few calls, ordering in a new nursing service for my dad. It's the least I can do. As I finish my call, my cell vibrates with a new text.

RACHEL: How was the ball?

Oh gods, the ball. Was it only last night? So much has changed. I was drugged, woke up in a strange castle, learned my company is worthless. And my father knew it. Everything he built was a lie.

I can't tell Rachel all this. I can't even wrap my own head around it.

"Good," I type, and bite my lip before deciding to distract her. You were right. Adam Archer is in to me.

RACHEL: Told you!!! Are you going to date him?

ME: We'll see. Right now I need some time away. I'll be gone a few days. Working on a breakthrough for Belladonna.

It's not a lie. If I can win the patents back, everything will be okay.

I'm putting Belladonna's future—my future—in the hands of a scary, possibly clinically insane, madman. But I don't have any other choice. Without the patents, Belladonna has zero assets. We don't own our research. There's no reason Archer Industries would want to merge with us. I have to get the patents back.

My phone starts ringing. Rachel, calling. Probably confused.

ME: Can't talk right now—

Before I hit send, I see a new message from an unknown number. Rejecting Rachel's call, I click on it.

UNKNOWN: Time's running out, Daphne.

Sure enough, the sun is sinking behind the skyscrapers.

It's time to head back to the Beast.

SIX

Beast

MY LEGS ARE stiff from standing at the window, waiting. Will she come? Or will she, like her father, try to find a way to worm out of her responsibilities and lash out like a child?

Well, they won't find me the weakling I once was. I've prepared for every outcome. If she makes any move other than submission, everything's in place.

I'll bury them.

You should have already. Giving her this opportunity out of sentimentality only proves you are still weak.

I slam the wall and turn away from the window. No. It's not sentimentality. I only punish the guilty. I, unlike the rest of this fucked up world, am just.

I laugh humorlessly. Because maybe that's all bullshit. Maybe I just want her for myself. Because I've watched her. I've watched them all as I've plotted my revenge. They all played out their roles over the years exactly as I would have expected.

All except her.

After the influx of capital from selling me the patents, her father expanded the company into cosmetics, made hundreds of millions, setting them up for the merger with Archer Industries. But little Daphne stayed buried away in her basement lab, working away into the wee hours of morning night after night working on the cure for Battleman's. Determined to find the cure for the disease that killed her mother.

But are her motives really so pure? Or when put to the test, will she disappoint like every other single human being on this earth?

I so hope to have the chance to find out.

I pace back to the window. "Come on, little girl. The sun is setting. Not much time now. What are you willing to do to save your company? Your precious research?"

The sun drops lower in the sky, and with it, my hopes.

I don't know why I'm so disappointed. I thought I'd lost all capacity for disappointment at this point in my life, but still, it hits me like a slug to the guts. I grab a vase from a stand nearby and throw it against the wall, turning away from the window.

At the same time I hear the roar of a car engine below.

I whip back around to look out the window. The car pulls to a stop on the circle drive right in front of the mansion and her tiny, waif-like body steps tentatively out. A masculine thunder of satisfaction floods my chest.

She's here. She came.

I'll teach her she's so much more than what they made her.

But first I have to break the mold of who she is so she can be reborn.

SEVEN

Daphne

THE WIND PICKS up as the taxi pulls away, leaving me in front of the castle. The stone face rises up stark and beautiful. *My new home. For however long it takes.*

I can't believe I'm here. I can't believe I'm doing this. My comfortable work shoes scuff the fancy patterned stonework as I work up the nerve to grab the heavy brass door knocker. Shaped like a demonic beast head, of course.

I can't believe I'm about to throw myself on the mercy of a madman to save my company. But Belladonna and my research are my life. Without them, what do I have left? Who am I?

A crisp ringing cuts the air. I leap about ten feet, fumbling for my cell phone. Adam's calling. My thumb hovers over the screen. Should I answer? Shit, I disappeared from the ball. I owe him an explanation.

Tucking myself into the archway to get out of the wind, I raise the phone to my ear. "Hello, Adam."

"Daphne! There you are. I've been so worried." My phone beeps, belatedly telling me I have several missed calls. I kept it off for most of the day, only turn it on at the end of the drive to text Rachel again, telling her not to worry. I meant to turn it off by now, but when my finger hovered over the power button, I couldn't bring myself to press it. Maybe I needed to feel connected to something familiar. Or maybe needing a way out—my last chance to call the cops.

"Sorry. I've been...distracted."

Adam says something but his words are all broken up.

"Adam? Can you hear me? The reception is going in and out." I step away from the building's stone face.

"Where are you?" Adam asks. "We need to talk. Are you at your apartment? Or the lab? I'll come get you."

"Um, no, I'm not home or at Belladonna. Listen, I'm taking a few days off. I working on...something. Something important." Were those footsteps beyond the door? I've got to explain things to Adam before the Beast shows up. "I've got to go—"

"Daphne, please listen. I need to apologize."

Apologize to me? "What?" The door creaks and I turn away.

"I didn't mean to scare you. All those things I said—I've been wanting to say them for a long time."

My mouth falls open. I can't believe this is happening now. The door yawns open behind me, filled with shadow.

"I know you're not experienced in these things," Adam says. "We can take it slow—"

"Adam, I really, really can't talk about this right now. If you'd just—"

A large hand closes over mine, snatching my cell phone out of my grasp. The hand grips it so hard the screen cracks, then lets it fall to the stone floor. A polished shoe kicks it onto the lawn.

I gape as the Beast looms over me. "Oh my gods! You're crazy."

The Beast lunges forward.

EIGHT

Beast

"PLEASE," Daphne begs. "I came like you said. What are you going to do to me?"

I tug her along, ignoring her pleas. I'd prepared a room for her, full of warmth and comfort. I thought she might not be tainted, too far gone. She might deserve better than her cheating father and lying lover.

I was wrong. She's just like them. She deserves nothing. She dares to come to me with *his* name on her lips? She deserves every punishment I've planned.

Her cries echo down the hall as I drag her to the stairs. Her purse falls to the floor, its contents scattering.

"Stop this!" she screams.

Her glasses go flying. She fights harder until I catch her wrists and draw her close.

"Stop. I can't see," she pants. She's always been a little nearsighted. Has her eyesight gotten worse? She stares up at my face, her gaze vague, confused.

Once she looked at me with affection. Awe. No more. Never again.

Because of him.

Growling, I bend at the waist and toss her over my shoulder. She pounds on my back, which has as much effect as a sparrow fighting a storm. I take the stairs two at a time. My heart pumps like bellows, the heat of my rage spreading through me.

I don't stop until I'm at the top of the tower. There's a prison here, a cage I designed especially for her. I hadn't thought to use it so soon, but...

"Welcome to your new home." I tell her, easing her down to the floor. As soon as she catches her bearings, she flies at me, but I clang the door shut.

In the dim light, she squints at me. I wait for her eyes to widen, some sign of recognition. But her features twist in anger.

"I knew you were crazy." She grasps the bars, her body shaking. With emotion or cold? The tower is chilly, and with the sun going down, the temperature will only drop.

I turn away before I grow weak, start feeling pity for my captive.

"This was a mistake," she mutters half to herself. "I should've gone to the cops!"

I pause on the top step. "Why didn't you?"

"I thought I could talk to you. Make you see reason." Her voice sounds so woeful, I clench my fists to keep from returning, unlocking the door. We could sit like we used to. I could explain everything...

No. She and her father showed me no mercy. Now it's her turn to suffer.

"Too late for that, princess," I tell her, and leave her shivering in the cold.

NINE

Daphne

WHEN I WAS A GIRL, I'd play at being princess. While my mother worked in her garden, I'd romp around, pretending the rose bushes were my castle. I imagined lush rooms with roaring fireplaces and floor-to-ceiling windows with views to beautiful gardens. My imaginary castle also boasted a fully-equipped laboratory. Because even when I played princess, I still was a scientist.

I never imagined I'd find myself in an actual castle. Much less locked in a tower.

Correction: locked in a cage inside a tower. Floor-to-ceiling bars mark the boundaries of my prison.

Wind whistles around the turret, setting my teeth on edge. The sound is un-ending, along with the cold. Winter came early this year.

I tuck my feet under me, but it's no use. The flagstones are freezing. It rained a little last night, and the water that seeped in froze before dawn.

Things got a little better when the sun got high, but now it's sinking again. Along with my hopes.

I press my forehead to my knees, shivering. I should've worn something thicker than leggings and a light sweater. My chest feels hollow and my head aches. The start of a cold or something more sinister? My immune system isn't strong at the best of times, and the stress of the past few days and this chill isn't helping.

My only hope is the brutal Beast, who dragged me here in the first place. But he's obviously a few bats short of a belfry.

Why am I always so sure I can fix things? That people will listen to logic? Life isn't a science problem. You can't always come up with a logical hypothesis and expect people to react in predictable ways to achieve desirable outcomes. Even science rarely works that way. Some problems take decades and longer to solve. There's too much chaos in the world.

And the Beast is the perfect expression of chaos made flesh.

A heavy step on the stair makes me lift my head. The Beast appears, his mask firmly in place. What does it hide? I wish I had my glasses. His hair looks thick and lush, but I could be wrong. I've never seen him clearly.

When he catches me staring, his dark eyes flash. He glares back. But I'm used to it.

The key clinks in the lock and the door slides against the flagstones, admitting a shiny pair of shoes. The Beast dresses well, at least. Tailored slacks, expensive sweater over a dress shirt.

Jailor-chic.

I remain curled in a ball, unwilling to give up any of my body heat to greet my guest.

He sets a tray down on the floor a foot in front of me.

"Dinner is served." His voice is deep, slightly raspy. Somehow familiar. I search my memory but I'm cold and tired and on my best day I'm not good at placing names and faces. Besides, no one I know is as big as this guy, wears a mask, or is completely psychotic.

I peer at the food he brought—some bread and a bowl of water. There's a skim of ice on the water's surface.

The blurry face of the Beast studies me a moment. Waiting for me to beg for mercy?

Holding my gaze, he slides the door shut. The lock clicks home.

"You think this will break me?" I blurt before I can stop myself. "I can handle cold and hunger. But if the temperature drops much more, I might not survive the night." I can list the exact effects of exposure on the body, but I bite my tongue.

"I won't let that happen."

"Forgive me if I don't trust a word you say."

"I'm not the one who's broken my word." He starts to turn away.

I launch myself at the bars, wincing as my fingers close around the cold metal. "I can't give you what you want if you don't tell me what it is!"

He stops with a foot on the stairs. "I want you to be the girl you once were. One who keeps her promises."

"I keep my promises. All my life, all I've ever done is what I'm supposed to do." What my father expected of me.

"You did what they wanted you to."

"Is that so wrong?" I throw my hands up in the air. "My research will save lives."

"Not if I destroy your company." His lips curl under the

mask. Such a cruel smirk. So why does his mouth mesmerize me?

He descends a few more steps. I slump to the floor. "You want me to become someone I never was. My father shaped me to follow in his footsteps. Continue his research. You want someone who was pure, untainted? You should've met my mother."

"I did." He hasn't moved, hasn't descended any lower. His face is on the same level as mine.

"You knew her?" I press my face against the bars, ignoring the chill. "Tell me how you knew her!" It's been years since she's died, but I'm hungry for any memory I can get.

"She was kind to me. When few people were."

"She was like that." I try to study his features behind the mask. "Wait. Were you in love with her?"

His forehead creases. He takes a moment to answer, as if considering my question. "I loved her as a child loves a mother. As a prodigal son loves the parent who welcomes him home."

"Then who hurt you? How can I know what I did if you don't tell me?" I mumble, staring at the floor. He wants humble? I can do humble. It's getting hard to hold myself up and the flagstones look soft.

My skin feels numb. Frostbite setting in? Soon I won't feel anything at all.

"You made a promise, then you broke it." Suddenly, he's looming over me. The bars are gone. "But now it's time for you to make amends."

The Beast is carrying me. He lifted me easily into his arms and strides smoothly down the spiral staircase. Guess his size isn't just for show. I'm too tired to fight, so I nestle in his arms, resting my face on the soft cashmere.

The further away from the tower, the warmer it gets. I relax.

"I was right," he mutters. "You have no tolerance for suffering."

"I've suffered. You have no idea."

"You grew up in the lap of luxury." He scoffs as he glides us through another door and down another staircase. "I've seen Thornhill."

He knows my family's home?

"Just because we lived in a big house didn't mean we had the means to heat it." We pass a massive fireplace and I struggle upright in his arms, drawn to the fire like a moth to a flame.

In an unusual act of kindness, the Beast sets me down on the carpet in front of it. Immediately I hold my hands out to the blaze.

"I remember winters at Thornhill," I tell the Beast. He grabs a large, heavy looking chair with a back higher than he is, and drags it over like it weighs nothing. Seating himself, he motions me to go on.

"My father would scrounge the forest for wood to burn in the fireplace. My mother would heat stones on the hearth, and tuck them in bed with me, to warm my feet." One of those bricks sounds great about now. My fingers tingle painfully as they warm up. I blink back tears.

The Beast leans forward and captures my hand in his. His large fingers are surprisingly gentle as he rubs life back into mine.

I realize I'm kneeling at the Beast's feet while he holds my hand. Up close, I can see the mottled skin at the edge of his mask. Some scarring. Is he a war victim? Was his flesh burned? Did he use a medicine my company invented and suffer horrible side effects? Is that what all this is about?

His dark eyes challenge mine and I dart my gaze away, clearing my throat.

"So, yeah, that was life at Thornhill. It was hard, but it was home."

He releases me, sitting back in the chair. With his long fingers steepled in front of his face and profile gilt in firelight, he looks like a monarch in repose.

And I'm the supplicant at his feet. I don't like sitting here, but my legs are too stiff for me to move.

Or I could pretend we're a happy couple, just back from a walk in our winter garden. He built up this fire for me like my dad used to, and we'll stay up late, lounging in front of it together...

"What are you thinking about?" I ask when the silence stretches. I can't forget he's my captor, and I'm at his mercy. Any chance to get in his head, I should take it.

Not fantasize that we're a couple, ala Stockholm Syndrome.

"I'm surprised your father didn't sell out sooner." I must be used to his deep voice, because it's soothing. "He would've done anything for your mother."

"Yes. But he couldn't. His research was her only hope." I flinch as I always do when talking about my mother's disease. The Beast is studying me so I quickly add, "Besides, we didn't need more than what we had. We had each other."

"A touching story." he sneers at the fire. "I suppose love kept you warm?"

I raise my chin. "I don't expect you to understand."

"I understand perfectly. Your mother died. Your father turned into a shell of his former self."

I flinch with each denouncement as if he's struck me.

"Is that why you no longer remain true to your vow?"

"What vow?" I cry out, finding the strength to rise to my knees.

"To remain pure." He seizes my shoulders. "Tell me, Daphne, why, after all these years, do you whore yourself for a rich man?"

I twist out of his hold. "I don't whore myself to anyone. I don't know what you're talking about."

"No? The nights out? The fine dining, the symphony? When did you spread your legs for him… after he gave you this?" He grasps the necklace I wear. The chain digs into my neck and I cry out, flailing at his arms.

"Stop it! My mother gave me this, you…you Beast."

"Beast." He lets me go and I fall back, tucking the rose charm away. "Fitting. I suppose that's how you see me."

"You're crazy." My voice is shaking. I was stupid to let down my guard with him, even for a second. "You're a Beast because you act like one." I run a hand through my hair. Why am I even bothering to explain? "I don't care how you look."

He tilts his head. I stare until his features blur, wishing again for my glasses. Something about his face is familiar…

"Don't care about looks?" he asks bitterly. "Only how much money a guy has?"

I raise my chin. "You don't know me."

"I know you better than anyone else does." His words echo in my head, triggering deja vu. I tilt my head, chasing the memory, but it disappears.

"What do you know about me?" At some point in the past moments, I've taken his hand. He turns my pale one over his, studying it as if it's a bird flown into his hands, fragile and precious.

"You've always tried to be what your father wanted. But you're more than that."

I close my eyes, remembering another time, another moment, another man telling me these things. But that man was kind, gentle. Nothing like the Beast.

"What did my father want me to be?"

"Hope. A lifeline. A savior. But he failed."

I flinch, drawing my hand back.

"You both did."

I stare at the fire. "You're speaking of my mother."

"Yes."

"We tried to save her."

"It wasn't your burden."

"Yes it is."

"Why? Because you can profit from it?" he sneers.

"What happened to you?" I ask, rising up on my knees before him. "Who hurt you?"

His face hardens. "They took everything from me."

"Who? My father?" When he doesn't answer, I add, "Adam?"

Large hands close over my shoulders, shaking me hard. "Do not speak his name!" he roars.

"Please," I cry. "I'm not with Adam. I never have been."

"Don't lie to me." Now the Beast is on his feet, tugging me up. Oh gods, will he put me back in the tower?

"Please, I just want to understand—" I plead as he drags me down the hall. Past the door that leads to the tower. I relax, only to stiffen again when he drags me to another door, and down a dark staircase. The temperature begins to drop again. "You're scaring me!"

"He won't ever have you."

"Where are you taking me?" I all but shriek as he leads me down the freezing stone corridor, holding my upper arm in a vice grip.

"Finding out the truth since I can't trust a word from

your lips," he growls, shoving open a heavy wooden door and dragging me into a dark room.

He lets go of me only once we're inside. For a second, I'm left breathing hard in the pitch black. Gods, does he mean to lock me in here?

But then he flips on the lights.

"On the bed," he demands.

I freeze. Every muscle in my body freezes. "Y-You're not serious," I stutter as I take in the stark, almost medieval looking room. Stone floors. Stone walls. The only exception to the monastery design?

The medical bed in the center of the room. Complete with restraints.

He gets in my face, his dark brown eyes burning. "Just how far are you willing to go to save your father's company?"

I glare up at him. "You want me to say it's okay for you to tie me down and rape me?"

"No," he chokes out, sounding furious. "I'm a doctor and I want you to prove you haven't been whoring yourself out to Adam Archer, as you claim."

My mouth drops open as he continues. "You can walk out that door right now if you want, princess." His massive arm shoots out and points towards the door we just came in through.

Damn him. Gods damn him.

"You're a sick fuck," I spit in his face. And then I stomp towards the bed and lay down, my arms crossed stubbornly over my chest.

There's a beat of silence, and then his footsteps sound on stone as he follows. I force myself not to close my eyes as he looms over me. The other thing about the room that's modern: the lights overhead. There's plenty of light.

So much light that when the Beast—what I've taken to calling him in my head—reaches into a cabinet underneath the bed and pulls out scissors, I can see exactly what he's doing.

And when he proceeds to reach for the hem of my sweater and starts to cut it up the middle, I know *he* can see all of *me* as he exposes me to the open air.

My eyes shoot to his as my breaths get shorter but he seems suddenly calm. Clinical? No, just extremely focused on what he's doing, I think. This is officially the craziest freaking thing that I've ever done in my life. How the hell did I get myself into this situation?

I'm not sure of anything at the moment, but before I even really wrap my head around what's happening, he's opened my top and exposed my bra.

My breath hitches and his eyes finally move up and meet mine. All the hostility from moments earlier is gone. There's...gentleness there? No, that can't be right. He's a beast. A monster who's threatening everything—

"I won't hurt you," he says, his voice still gruff but softer than I've ever heard it. And then his huge, warm hand takes my wrist, drawing my arm away from my body. He peels my now open sweater off of my arm and then, slowly, gently, his eyes still on mine, he lifts my arm above my head and secures it in a padded wrist restraint.

He leans in close as he does it and when I next breathe in, all I inhale is...*him.* Pine and leather, but warmed by his body heat...it's like nothing I've ever smelled before. My body wakes up at the scent and I blink in confusion as he secures my other wrist.

"W-why do you have to tie me down?" I ask breathily, trying to gather my wits back.

"No questions," he says and I'm stupidly relieved at

his answer. What if for once, for once in my whole stupid life, I didn't question everything to death? What if...what if I just let this...happen? Would it really be so bad to just, I don't know, give up trying to control everything for once?

So I don't complain or question as he moves down my body with those damnable scissors of his and cuts my leggings off. The soft material gives easily and soon he's pulling the shredded material from my body. I shiver, left only in my panties and bra. It's cold in the room, there's no denying that. But...I don't think that's where the soul-deep quiver is coming from.

I've never been naked in front of a man before.

The Beast can think whatever he wants, but I'm a virgin in every sense of the word. I've never done...*anything*. Ever.

And his eyes aren't gentle looking anymore. They're heated and his nostrils flare as his eyes scan up and down my body. He's looking at me like...like the way a man looks at a woman. He's not trying to hide it. He wants me. Wants me like *that*.

He runs his huge hand down my thigh, pausing on my knee, and then down my calf to my ankle. My ankle has never looked more petite or delicate than when in his giant hand.

I can only watch, mesmerized for some reason, as he pulls out stirrups from the bottom of the bed and sets my left foot in them, and then repeats the same ritual with my right. I've never been so, well, *manhandled,* before.

You should be afraid right now. You should be kicking and screaming.

But his touch continues to be delicate as he skims his fingertips back up my leg, and then up the hollow of my stomach, between my ribs, and finally to my sternum and up to the little bow on the front of my bra in the valley between my medium-sized breasts.

My breath hitches again—good gods, have I taken a full breath since he put his hands on me?—as his deft fingers undo the snap right above the tiny silver bow. The next second, my breasts spring free and my nipples immediately pucker in the cold air.

He's standing close enough that I can hear *his* breath catch. And he's so solid, so huge, so masculine and warm and so sure in his movements—it's ridiculous to be comforted by him... But I am. I'm naked and vulnerable and he's clothed and warm and my body instinctively turns towards him.

His eyes shoot towards mine, obviously surprised at my movement. Yeah, buddy, me too. I blink but don't look away. He's the one to break eye contact first, but I quickly discover it's only so he can get back to his work. I soon hear the snip of the scissors again and then my panties, my last bit of coverings, are falling away.

Instinctively, I try to lock my knees together but the Beast whispers, "Shhh, open to me like the beautiful rose you are."

And then his hands, those sinful hands of his, are skimming down my thighs again. Except that this time, they move right back up along the *inside* of my thighs as he moves around the bed from my side to—I suck in a deep gulp—to in between the stirrups.

His huge hands gently caress my knees.

Then he pries them apart.

And I let him. Oh gods, I let him.

His thumbs immediately go *there*. To my...my private places. I jerk in my restraints as his thumbs massage along the outer lips of my...my *sex*.

"I'd prefer to use your natural lubricant to examine you," he murmurs. "Give me your juices, Daphne."

I nod because I don't trust myself to manage words. But to be honest, I'm not completely sure what he's talking about. I mean, I sort of know the biology of, well, *sex*. My face flushes even thinking the word. But I just don't— I mean, I don't have time for that sort of—

Okay, so a couple of times I tried touching myself but I'm usually so tired and I was never sure if I was doing it right anyway. So I always gave up before anything really happened. There were always so many more important things to attend to anyway. Who cared if I never figured out sex when I was trying to save people's lives?

But the Beast's fingers aren't clumsy like mine were the couple times I attempted to touch myself. He's sure, in command, and more than that, demanding as one hand continues to play with my sex and the other presses flat up my stomach back to the valley of my breasts. But this time, he strays from the beaten path.

He cups my breast. I'm dwarfed in his hand, but when his thumb strums over my nipple I don't feel lacking. My back arches off the table into his touch and as if it's instinctual, he pinches my nipple harder.

And that lubricant he was talking about? It fairly gushes all over his other hand.

"That's right," he growls, sounding more like his old self as the hand at my sex probes between my now-soaking folds.

My breaths come in short, shallow pants. "What's happening?" Pleasure shoots from my breast to my sex and my stomach liquifies and swoops. Gods, I've never felt anything like this before.

His hand grips my breast harder. "Don't mock me. No one's that innocent."

But the more pressure he applies, the more the pleasure intensifies. My hands ball into fists and I want to scream at him to keep touching me, to keep going. My sex clenches as his thick forefinger teases at my entrance.

I think... I think I want him to push his finger inside. I want something inside me. He strums his thumb across the flesh about an inch above the opening and if I thought I was on fire before, "Oh!" I cry, a shudder wracking my body. No, I don't just want something inside me to clench around, I *need* it. I've never— This is—

"Please," I whimper, not really knowing what I'm begging for, but knowing he can give it to me.

Through slitted eyes, I see confusion on his face, but then his expression hardens and he gives me what I've asked for.

He plunges a finger inside me.

It hurts and feels amazing at the same time. I blink at all the sensations assaulting me. A man has his fingers inside me. He's penetrating me. He's...he's finger-fucking me. I shudder at the dirtiness of the thought and the feel of his digit impaled inside me.

"Daphne," he cries, voice choked. "You're a virgin."

I want to laugh. He sounds so shocked.

"I know," is all I say.

Though, am I still technically a virgin now? I mean, did his finger rupture my hymen? He shoved it in so forcefully.

I clench around his finger. I've become acclimated to it and now I want him to move it. If he did break my hymen, then surely this was much nicer than having a huge cock do the work—surely that would hurt a lot more. This was just a short little pinch and now I want him to explore.

"Fuck, you're tight," he whispers, starting to remove his finger.

"Don't," I whisper and his eyes shoot to mine. I can't quite bear that. This is all too new, I'm feeling too many things. Eye contact seems like too much.

But still, I manage to continue. "Not yet?" It comes out as more of a question and then I stupidly follow it up with, "um...please?"

But the reward comes so quickly I'll happily beg again. Besides, when was the last time I asked for something I wanted? Something just for me? But this...this is a space out of time, out of my regular life.

The finger inside me begins to move. Slowly. Languorously.

"You'll get your reward now," he whispers. "You'll get your reward for staying pure for me. Tell me, little Daphne, do you touch yourself when you're all alone in the dark?"

I shake my head. "A couple of times, but it never felt like this."

His nostrils flare again. "Good girl. Good, good girl. You never touch yourself. I'm the only one who touches you. *Ever*. Do you understand? I'm the only one who touches this pretty, pretty pussy."

My sex clenches around his finger at the dirty word. *Pussy*. Another shudder of pleasure runs through me.

"Oh, you like that," he croons. "You want me to master your pussy and your pleasure. Your sweet little cunt is so creamy for me."

And then he leans down between my legs and inhales. Aghast at his action, I try to shove my legs together but his huge, broad shoulders are wedged between my legs and it's no use.

"Uh uh uh," he chastises me. "I'll smell your sweet cunt all I want. I'll wake up, tie you down, and lap at your delicious smelling cunt for breakfast if I want to. And you'll let me, won't you. You'll beg me to."

I've never heard such filthy words in my entire life. And the way my body responds? Oh *gods*. I'd be embarrassed if he didn't seem to be getting off on my every reaction, too.

Every little whimper I make, he inhales and his chest seems to expand even more, as impossible as that seems since he's already so huge.

But it's like he's feeding off my energy, and the synergy we're creating is the most intense thing I've ever experienced. It's a high I didn't know could exist, and I can't escape the whirlwind—don't want to escape, oh gods, I never want to come down.

Especially because it's still ramping *up*. That slow, torturous finger moving in and out of me plus his thumb, *oh*, that wicked, wicked thumb of his, plus the hand massaging my breast and tweaking my nipple—I thought it was a myth that breasts could arouse a woman. But I was wrong. Oh, I was so, *so* wrong.

And everything he's doing to me is so, so right.

"Yes," I cry out, grinding my hips into his hand in an instinctual motion as my mouth goes dry from panting. "Please, *yes*."

"That's right," he grinds out, "beg for it. Beg for me."

"Please, *please*." My hands clench around the material of my restraints. I have to grab something, need *something* to ground me as my body spirals out of my control. It's *his*, he's the commander and master of my body now. It's going where he takes it.

He leans between my legs and inhales my scent and it's

the dirtiest and hottest thing I've witnessed yet, this godly, masculine man of all men, scenting me at my most secret place. And then he breathes out on me, blowing the warm air from his lungs in a warm stream across my sex, making me tremble. He redoubles his efforts on the bundle of nerves at the top of my sex at the same time he massages me deep within and it's too much— It's—

"*Ohhhhh!*" I cry as the volcano that's been stewing inside me finally erupts.

I want to clench him to me as white light engulfs me and shock waves blast outwards from my center, singeing me from my scalp to the tips of my fingertips and toes.

One wave...and then another and...oh gods *another*.

My legs spasm as yet one more wave hits. The restraints hold me down so all I can do is look at my Beast with all the longing and euphoria I feel.

His eyes are wide and satisfied and...shocked.

I don't think he expected this any more than I did.

As the last bit of pleasure spasms and then ekes out of my body, my limbs sink limp to the table and I feel like I've expended every ounce of energy I ever had. But it's not like at the end of an exhausting all-nighter at the lab. I feel... sated. And so, *so* satisfied. Like, I didn't even know the meaning of the word satisfaction before this moment.

I breathe out every ounce of tension and sink into the table, goosebumps rising from the cold hitting my sweat-drenched body. I couldn't care less.

For once in my life, all my thousands of worries and concerns are quiet. It's so blissfully quiet in my head. I sink into the beautiful silence. Gods, I want to live here. I'm so tired of carrying everything. I want to just put it all down.

So I sink into the silence, so much so that I barely feel the hands undoing the restraints on my wrists and ankles.

And when my Beast gathers me into his arms and carries me from the room, I sink against *him*, my mind still blissfully quiet as I listen to the solid *thump thump thump* of his heart in his huge, warm chest.

TEN

Beast

THAT DIDN'T GO AS PLANNED. She wasn't supposed to be a virgin. I was so sure she wasn't a virgin. That she was a liar, just as corrupt as the rest of them.

But I was wrong. I was so wrong.

She's a rarity, a hardy winter rose among flashier summer blooms, made of sterner stuff and all the more beautiful for it. And the way she unfurled before my eyes...

"That's it, sweetheart," I whisper into the silky fall of her hair. Hours of freezing torture in the tower, and she's as beautiful as ever, her olive skin flushed from the pleasure I gave her, if a bit smudged from sleeping on the dirty stone. "Time to clean you up."

She murmurs a protest when I set her down in the tub.

I turn the gold knobs and test the water temperature until it's perfect. There's a new cake of soap waiting to be unwrapped. Rose scented, of course. I lather a soft washcloth and place it between her legs. She winces with a little moan.

"Sore?" My deep voice echoes around the bathroom and brings a deeper flush to her cheeks.

Biting her lip, she nods.

"Was that the first time you've had something inside you?" I still can't believe she's a virgin.

She raises her chin, looking regal even though she's wet and naked. "That's none of your business."

Still that fire in her eyes even as she gave in to me so beautifully. My cock is hard as a rock from just remembering her sweet submission.

I growl and pull her hands away from where they cover her breasts. "Everything about you is my business. You belong to me now, Daphne."

"I don't belong to anyone. I'm my own person."

"Really? Is that why you've worked so hard to be a clone of your father?" *And Adam Archer*, I add silently, though I won't say that fucker's name. Maybe I don't have to kill him now, since he hasn't defiled my precious rose.

It wasn't supposed to be about her. It was supposed to be about revenge...but now. After having her here, after watching her shatter beneath me, inhaling her virgin scent as she detonated in her first ever orgasm that *I* and I alone wrung from her—

To my surprise, she gnaws her lip. "That's also personal."

I catch her chin. "You're not theirs any longer. You're mine." This is the only thing I've become absolutely sure of over the past hour.

She's changing everything.

But it doesn't mean I can't have my revenge still.

She will be my revenge now. I will take Dr. Laurel's

daughter and make her *mine*. I will snatch the woman Adam Archer wants right out from under his nose. When I'm done with her, she'll crave no one else but *me*.

Except maybe...maybe I'll never be done with her. If she continues to be what she appears, if she really is *pure*, then...

I gaze down at the perfect beauty, naked before me. Steam rises from the tub and she groans in pleasure. Can she really be all she appears to be? There's so much more of her to explore. Not just her body, but her mind.

The tub is one of the few modern accoutrements I've added to the place, along with all the modern plumbing and lighting. One of the few pleasures I allow myself. It's large and when I reach over and turn on the jets, Daphne murmurs happily.

Other than her few spitfire moments since we finished earlier, she's mostly been like a sleepy cat. She reaches for me again and again, and I have to capture her wrists before she tries to dig her paws into my chest.

I'll have to train my kitten, won't I? No touching her Master.

Only I do the touching.

But she's had enough lessons for today.

So I gently wash her. She tries to cover herself, but I *tsk* and pull her hands away. After a moment, her raven head sinks back against the tall edge of the tub.

"What am I doing?" she whispers, more to herself than to me. "This is so wrong."

"Why?" I ask, sifting my hands through her long, dark, silky hair. I pour some shampoo into my hand. I added a feminine sounding shampoo to my grocery order yesterday and the scent of roses soon fills the bathroom. She leans forward when I direct her, bowing her head.

I love the shape of her tiny, delicate skull in my hands as I massage the suds in. So much life embodied in such a fragile container. And her amazing brain. I know just how smart Daphne Laurel is.

That she has the capacity for such genius and also such beautiful submission... My hands tremble as I continue to wash her hair and I'm glad she's facing away so she can't see.

"What do you mean, *why*?" she asks. "You're my, my *captor*," she sputters.

I purse my lips and continue to massage her scalp. "Or we're two consenting adults and for a while you're deciding to give your power over to me. You're just realizing how good it feels to lay it down. To let me take care of you."

I slide one suds-slippery hand down her neck and down the front of her chest to her breast and lean close. "Maybe you realize how *good* it feels to be bad. To let go." I bite at her ear, and it's more than just a nibble.

She gasps and her nipples that have only been pebbled before turn hard as rocks, peeping out just above the roiling jet water.

"What's so wrong about that?" I continue whispering in her ear before pulling away and sliding my hand back up into her hair.

She's left panting and I smile. No one's ever reacted to me the way she has...but maybe that's the point, too.

I'm only able to be my true self with her. Only with each other are we able to be our true selves.

Only with each other are we able to be free.

She doesn't say anything else as I pour pitchers of warm water over her head to wash out the shampoo.

I continue talking and washing her sweet, petite little

body. "That's right. Let go. I'll take care of everything. You don't have to do a thing."

I lift her arm and run just the tips of my fingers up and down her forearm, then up to her biceps. I brush a bar of pink soap underneath her armpit and she giggles and drops her arm back down.

It's the most precious and adorable sound and I immediately want to hear it again, so I pull her arm up and repeat the motion. Her giggle is even more high-pitched this time. She squirms and splashes, trying to get away from me.

She flips like a fish in my arms but I'm even quicker, grabbing her wrists and pinning them to the sides of the tub as I flip, too, looming over her. Water droplets gleam like gemstones on her eyelashes and she's still laughing but she quickly sobers, her eyes searching mine back and forth.

"Will you take off the mask?" she asks, breathless. "I want to see you."

If there's one thing that could sour my mood, it's that question.

"No, you don't," I bark, pulling back, but only so that I can grab her by the waist and bend her over the side of the large tub.

"Elbows on the marble. On your knees." The tub has a wide marble lip on all sides and I indicate where she's to position herself.

Her eyes flash back up to mine uncertainly and I narrow mine at hers. This isn't a democracy. "Now," I order.

She nods and gets into position, knees in the water so that just her rear end peeks out of the water, arms on the wet marble. I frown. The marble might be uncomfortable on her elbows so I reach for a towel and place it underneath them. Her breath hitches—at my nearness or because she's thankful for the towel, I'm not sure.

Without thinking, I lay a hand on her spine and run it up and down—a gesture of comfort? No. I wouldn't know how. I just want contact with her. Every second I go without touching her feels wrong somehow.

All I know is my own body relaxes as soon as contact is reestablished. "That's a good girl," I murmur. "Such a good girl."

I grab a soft washcloth from the ledge and dip it into the soapy water. "I'm going to make you dirty, over and over. I'm going to make you such a filthy girl."

I run the hot, dripping cloth down her perfect, peach-plump ass and her back arches ever so slightly. Always so responsive.

"And then I'll clean you up so good."

I drag the cloth up the inside of her thigh beneath the water, emerging right at her sex. "I'll clean this sweet little pussy after you cum and squirt your filthy juices down your leg."

A shudder runs down her spine and my own cock lengthens. But this isn't about me. Not yet. I'll take this so slow, so achingly slowly, that she'll be begging me. And then I still won't give it to her.

A smile curves my lips. Oh, how I'm going to torture her. And not out of revenge. No, I'm going to torture her so that I become her only Master.

I'm going to initiate her into every pleasure she never imagined even existed. I'm going to introduce her to her own body, to her own desires, and finally, *finally*...maybe I'll even introduce her to me?

No. I immediately back away from the thought. It's enough to master her desires and her body. To deny *them*—those who have betrayed me—and keep her for myself.

Even if she never knows who I am.

ELEVEN

Daphne

I WAKE up and I'm so *warm*. Gods, I'd swear I'd been cold for years and to finally be warm, snuggled in the most comfortable bed with piles of blankets on me and my face warmed by— I frown and open my eyes slowly.

It *is* a fire!

I snap to attention and sit up, blankets falling off me as I do. There are no fireplaces in my extremely functional city apartment.

But no, of course, I'm not *in* the city anymore, am I? I've fallen through the looking glass. I look slowly around. It's far from the cold stone of the monastic room the Beast first thrust me into.

There's a huge, thick Persian rug on the floor, and on the window-sill, I shit you not, there's a legit bird just hanging out and *tweet-tweet-tweeting*. Um, when did I step into a fairytale movie? Then I giggle, my face flushing as I remember back to all the things that happened last night—definitely *not PG*.

I cover my face with my hands. Am I really at the stage where I can giggle about all this? What the hell is happening and can Dr. Daphne Laurel, PhD please return to the building?

Then I drag my hands back through my hair—hair that's extra soft from whatever girlie shampoo he used on it. I never think about stuff like that and just buy whatever's cheap and functional.

Let go. I'll take care of everything. You don't have to do a thing.

I wrap myself in a blanket and slide off the bed, padding to the window. The bird flies away when I press my forehead to the glass, staring down several stories of sheer greygreen stone. My chest cinches tight. I can't just *do* that. Let go. He doesn't know what he's asking. What seemed so natural in the moment feels impossible now. I *clench*. I've clenched all my life.

When Mom got sick. When Dad said it was up to us to save her. I clenched, got down to it and studied my ass off. Mom died and I clenched even harder, *hold it all in, don't let anyone see, Dad needs you, be strong for him, for all the people still struggling with Battleman's disease.*

Gods, I literally have to take medication for constipation I'm so damned clenched all the time. I know, sexy. It's just my normal.

Until him. Until last night.

I mean, the medical exam was one thing, but then there was the bath. He stayed clothed both times, but his hands on my body were as intimate as anything I've ever... My eyes drop closed at the memory of his caresses.

He did exactly what he said. Dirtied me, making me come over and over and then washing me only to flip me to another position in the tub and make me come another way. Until his touch felt like the most natural thing in the world. Until I was pruned and so exhausted, I barely remember him tucking me into bed like a sleepy, compliant kitten.

I step away from the window. My hand shakes as I brush my hair behind my ear. Then I look around for my hair tie. I always wear my hair in a bun. A tight bun.

Clench.

My hair tie is nowhere to be found. Neither is my purse where I always carry plenty of extras.

Instead my hair fluffs around me in an unruly mess. Not a complete mess. It's brushed. ...He brushed it last night before tucking me into bed.

The wave of relaxation that washes over me even at the memory of his touch calms some of the panic that's been creeping in...until that itself freaks me out. What the hell? Nothing relaxes me! Nothing and no one! I've tried everything. Meditation, wine, hot baths... but shit, thinking about baths just reminds me of last night, again.

I've got to get the hell out of here or I'm just gonna go nuts battling with my own thoughts. I'm exhausted and I just woke up. I'll go stir-crazy if I sit here much longer.

I pull on a soft sweater and another pair of thick leggings and socks and head for the door.

I pause when I reach out to touch it, sure it will be locked. Even after last night? Then I scoff at myself. *You think that changed anything? Really?*

But when I grab the knob, it turns easily.

Not locked.

I push through and then step out into the forbidding castle, squinting to see in the dimly lit corridor.

At the far end of the corner, light beams in diagonally from a high window, making dust motes dance in the air. But even as I walk towards it, the light falters and I hear thunder rumble overhead.

I shiver and think about calling out *hello?* But no, I'm not ready to see the Beast again so soon. Besides, how hard can it be to find the kitchen and get myself something to eat? My stomach rumbles, urging me on. This place might be big, but the kitchen will always be *down*, right? On the first floor or maybe the basement? That's how old places like this were built? Upstairs/Downstairs kinds of arrangements?

I wrap my arms around myself and when I come to the end of the corridor and open a heavy door to a stairwell that heads up and down, I hurry down the stairs.

Damn, my feet are freezing. I wish I had something more than socks. It just makes me hurry faster. I pass one landing and keep going down. I was on the second or third floor, right? I think so, judging from when I looked out the window earlier.

When I come to the landing for what I think is the first floor, I keep going down. This has to be a servant's stairwell, for as little frills as it has—I run my hand along down the railing as I go and then grimace—and as much dust has gathered. I take it the Beast doesn't have a cleaning staff or call in a service. I wipe my hands on my leggings as I get to the bottom of the stairs and the dust smears on the soft black fabric.

Finally I push through the door at the bottom of the stairwell and—

It's pitch black.

I gasp and stumble back, making sure the door doesn't close behind me. The last thing I need is for the door to shut and lock behind me and leave me down here lost in the dark.

But I catch the door and when I fumble along the wall, I easily find a light switch. Oh thank goodness.

My thumping heart slows down but then I step forward, curious.

It's a...gym.

Okay, not what I was expecting. But it helps explain the hulking muscles of my captor. *Captor? Really? Can you still call him that after last night?* You *were the one begging.*

Heat flares in my cheeks. Nope. Not thinking about that right now. Maybe not ever.

I walk closer to the weight bench and run my hand along the smooth, worn leather and then the stand of neatly stacked weights. There's also a treadmill, a stationary bike, and a rowing machine. Well, good to know I can still keep up my cardio if the Beast will let me borrow his toys.

I cross the stone floor to the door at the other end of the room. The lights from the gym spill into a dark hallway. I flip another switch and a light flickers lazily on overhead, just one for the entire hallway. It's the basement, so there aren't any windows here to help relieve the unrelenting darkness.

I should turn back. I'm not seeing any kitchen. And it's damp and cold down here. I can't feel my toes anymore. I should've just waited in my room. It's not like the Beast is going to starve me. He was probably about to bring me breakfast.

Then I scoff at my thoughts. Since when do I wait around for people to take care of me? I'm Dr. Daphne Laurel. I see problems and I fix them. My litany of failed experiments flash through my mind. Well, I *try* to fix them anyway. I *will* fix them, in the end. Starting with finding myself some freaking breakfast.

I straighten my shoulders and start down the hall. I stop at the first door I come to, doubting it's the kitchen but determined to check every one anyway. Learning more about my surroundings can only be a good thing.

I flip on the light and laugh. Seriously?

A bowling alley?

Okay, it's just one lane, but still, it looks regulation length, and there are pins set up in formation at the end and everything. I look around. Like, surely, this has gotta be some sort of joke.

But nope. The Beast loves...bowling? Or maybe it came with the place? Unlike the stairwell, though, there's no layer of dust here, and I walk over the smooth, polished wood floor to the stand of bowling balls. There are various weights on the balls, but all of them have *huge* finger holes. I slip my slim fingers inside them and they're engulfed. I yank my hands back. These are definitely the Beast's balls. Of course they're twice the average size. S*nicker*.

I step back and turn off the light, closing the door as quietly as I can behind me. I don't know why it feels like peeking in these two rooms; it seems like I'm seeing into an intimate part of the Beast's life. Parts he doesn't share with anyone else. Things maybe no one else in the world knows about him.

I back away from the door. But I don't turn and go back upstairs to my room. I head further down the hallway. I'm hungry for more. All I have are such incomplete pieces to the puzzle that is the man that's suddenly taken over my life. It's just a survival instinct. That's all.

Yeah, keep telling yourself that.

I bite my lip and glance into the next few rooms. Nothing but storage. Okay, so maybe there's nothing else to find anyway. It's just a basement after all. I'm surprised by a flash of disappointment.

When I come to the end of the hallway, I flip another light and gasp. It opens to an arched stone vestibule that's frankly fucking stunning. I step in, my eyes on the intricate corbels and vaulted ceiling so that it takes me a moment to take in what the room is being used for.

But finally my eyes drop back down to the huge open room...and all the very familiar equipment carefully set out on a neat array of lab tables.

Computers hum at several stations. There's a lab-grade DNA sequencer off to the left, set up incongruously beside a gothic stone column. My feet take me towards one of several electron microscopes and my inner lab geek takes over. I pull on lab gloves from a box underneath the table and then sit down at the little stool in front of one of the machines. I grab a slide from a set labeled 'specimens' and put it underneath the microscope.

It's a blood sample and when I turn on the microscope light and put my eyes to the eyepiece, the sight through the viewfinder is so familiar I gasp.

Battleman's? He's studying Battleman's disease?

I jerk back, bewildered. I don't understand. If he's interested in finding a cure for Battleman's—Belladonna's research is the best hope for a cure. Why would he interrupt my research like this? Potentially derail all our efforts and shut down our company? None of it makes any sen—

"What the *hell* are you doing here?" A roar comes from behind me.

I swing around on my stool. The Beast is towering behind me, the same way I entered the room.

I stand up. "What are *you* doing? Why didn't you tell me you're studying Battleman's? Why would you endanger my research? If you care about a cure, then you have to let me continue my—"

"Silence!" he shouts, the part of his face not covered by the mask red with rage. It's only then I start to realize the depth of my misstep and back away from him. Which is also apparently the wrong move because he only glowers at me and starts in my direction.

"You think you can run from me? You violate my privacy, take what's not yours as if it's your *right*? You're just like the rest of them after all!"

"That— That's not fair!" I sputter. "This disease killed *my* mother—"

"And you own the patent on suffering," he sneers. "I forgot."

"You're twisting everything I say!" I shout back. It's not fair. I was— I was just—

His eyes burn with dark fire and when his chest heaves up and down, it reminds me of a mountain—no, a volcano—and he looks like he's about to blow. "I think it's time for another lesson reminding you exactly where your place is."

And shit, as soon as his words sink in—

I run.

I just run. There's no thinking involved. It's fight or flight and all I apparently have the capacity for at the moment is *flight*.

I run the opposite direction out of the huge room. I don't know where I'm going. *Obviously* there's no thinking involved. Do I really think I can outrun the Beast? In his own fucking house? What the hell? What the hell what the hell what the hell? I manage to slam a light switch as I head into another corridor.

I careen down the long hallway, vaguely registering that the corridors correspond to the two wings of the castle above. Or am I just hoping that they're mirrors of each other and that there will be a stairwell at the end of this corridor, too? Yes, yes, I'm definitely hoping that.

"Don't you dare run!" the Beast roars from behind me. "It'll only be worse once I catch you!"

Oh fuck. I sprint faster, going all out, balls to the wall for the door at the end of the long hallway. I make the fatal mistake of looking over my shoulder. Oh *fuck!*

He's halfway down the corridor and gaining. I yank on the door, sure it's going to be locked. And sure enough, it doesn't open.

"No," I cry, and yank again. This time the door budges with a squeal of old hinges. Not locked! Just really old and probably warped in its frame. I wrench the door with my whole body and it opens. Just in time, too, because though I don't look behind me again, I can hear the Beast's footsteps and he's almost on top of me.

I don't bother searching for a light switch this time, I just flee up the stairs. There's no window in this stairwell so I'm running in the pitch dark but I don't care. I run faster than I've ever run before, taking the steps two at a time. But he has much longer legs than me and I know he'll catch up with me any second.

When I reach the first landing, I yank open the door and throw myself through. He's right behind me and, in for a penny in for a pound, I grab the closest thing I can find, a wing-backed chair, and shove it in front of the door.

The Beast immediately slams into the door right behind me and I screech. Should I try to put something else in front of the door or just keep running. He slams the door again and the chair topples.

I take off through the sitting room, chancing one glance back over my shoulder, sure he'll be right on top of me.

But when he toppled the chair, it landed on its side and wedged itself in the corner and blocked the door! He can't get the door open more than a few inches, no matter how many times he rams it with his huge body.

At least that's what I think...until the chair splinters and he bursts through. Shit, he's strong.

What the hell was I doing yesterday, letting myself cuddle up to such a violent man? He's blackmailing my father. He *tied me down* yesterday. This is not normal or sane.

I keep running. I have to get the hell out of this place. Screw everything I thought was keeping me here. This guy's a madman. He's fucking chasing me down like an animal. He's been lying to me. He wants things I don't understand, can't comprehend. I can't do this, any of this—

I see an exit, two double doors made of colorful panes of glass. Now that I'm back above ground, I can hear that the thunderstorm I suspected earlier is now in full swing. Lightning flashes through the windows. Good. Maybe it'll distract the Beast and I'll be able to get away. I need all the camouflage I can get.

I grab the long-handled knob and push through the door and out into the storm. It's mid-morning but the dark clouds overhead make it look like forbidding twilight. Rain lashes my face but I don't stop. I run down the stone steps and into a vast garden.

At least I think it's a garden... Until I stumble and slip on the mud as I enter through an iron lattice archway and find myself in...another fucking labyrinth.

"You've gotta be kidding me," I shout into the rain right as thunder booms overhead. But maybe I can hide inside, wait out the storm, and then escape? That's totally a possibility, right? Right?

In the heat of the moment, it makes sense to my frenzied mind, and besides, I'm already running and stumbling through the maze of bushes.

Rose bushes. They're freaking rose bushes. A hysterical laugh bubbles out of me. Of course they're rose bushes. Sagging under the weight of the raindrops. Red and white and pink blossoms flash on the periphery of my vision as I continue to rush headlong deeper into the labyrinth, turning left and then right, right, choosing at random whenever I come to a fork in the path.

"Daphne!" I hear the Beast's shout somewhere behind me, barely audible above the storm. "Stop this. It's not safe out here. Call out to me and we'll go inside!"

I scramble forwards at the sound of his voice, right into a rosebush. Thorns tear at my flesh and I yank back, only scratching myself worse as I try to disentangle myself from the brambles. The pain only adds to the sense of disorientation from the storm and the crazy adrenaline pumping through my veins. I stumble back and start running again. I thought adrenaline was supposed to make my mind think *clearer*. Where's my fucking clarity?

I don't know how long I keep running and stumbling through the maze but I never come to the end of it. I'm probably going in circles without even knowing it.

"Daphne! Stop this! It isn't safe, let me—" Thunder drowns out the rest of whatever he says. But he sounded closer than before.

I look over my shoulder...and my sweater catches on another rose bramble. Dammit! I rip my sweater to get away, again the thorns tear at my flesh. Lightning flashes right overhead and almost simultaneously, thunder booms.

That means the storm's right on top of us. I come to another fork in the path, sheets of rain coming down so hard that even if I hold my hand over my eyes, I still barely make anything out. The squelching mud beneath my feet tugged off my socks a long time back and my toes sink into the freezing mire.

I blink, suddenly dizzy, and so, *so* cold. How long have I been out here? My chattering teeth are a rat-a-tat-a-tat snare drum in my head. Have I ever been warm in my life? With the rain lashing me from above, and the sinking mud from below, it's suddenly hard to remember if I have.

Maybe when my mother was alive. But she's been gone a long time.

Dead. She's been *dead* a long time. Cold in the ground. She's so cold and I did nothing to save her.

I *failed* her. I'm still failing her. I'm failing everyone. I try so hard but it doesn't matter. Every day I wake up and think, maybe *this* will be the day, but it never is and now— Now—

I sink to my knees in the mud, and then lower. I drop my forehead to the mud, the forceful rain lashing my head from above forcing me even lower. Maybe I'll just finally join her and give up all this struggling. I can only fight for so long.

And suddenly all the fight's gone out of me. I'm as weak as a kitten. Even the thought of trying to get back up again and take another step feels like trying to climb Mount Olympus.

The cold creeps up my legs, from the outside in. *I'm coming home, Mom. I'm sorry.*

I close my eyes and give in to the cold.

"Daphne! Oh gods!"

And then suddenly, I'm being lifted, I'm flying. Is this

what it's like when the gods pick you up to carry you to heaven? Will I wake in the Elysian Fields with my mother, finally at peace? A smile crosses my face.

And then I pass out.

TWELVE

Beast

I SPRINT with her back into the house. She weighs nothing in my arms. Insubstantial. Beautiful and precious even covered in mud, more precious, because her shivering and clacking teeth mean she's still with me.

I run with her up the main staircase and straight to the bath. I cradle her in my arms as I start the shower in the corner. It's custom made, big enough for two with double shower heads. I turn on both of them to full blast. As soon as the water is even moderately warm, I climb in with her. We're both wearing clothes and filthy but I don't care.

Nothing matters except getting her warm.

"Come on, baby," I whisper, rubbing my hands up and down her arms. "Come on, warm up for me. Can you hear me? Give me a nod if you can hear me."

Her eyes open to mere slits but she nods as steam starts to fill the bathroom when the water finally heats. I run my hand under the jet of water.

"Fuck," I hiss. Too hot. I don't want to send her into shock, either, so I turn down the temperature. We should go slow.

I turn it to a moderately hot temperature and then arrange her under the spray. She jerks and tries to turn away from it but I hold her steady. "Shh, it's alright. Everything's gonna be alright now. I'll take care of you. I swear it. Just give into the warmth. Let it seep into you."

And it's like those are the magic words, or maybe it's just my voice she's responding to, because she turns and curls into my arms like it's the most natural place in the world for her to be. My breath hitches but I don't stop.

I peel her soaked, filthy sweater off over her head and she lets me, then curls right back into my chest. And then she just nestles there. Like I'm her safe place in the storm.

Ha. Right. She ran away from you *into* the storm.

If she'd been out there even five more minutes... What the fuck was she *thinking*?

But I know, don't I? I remember the look of fear on her face before she turned and fled—and that after standing up so magnificently to me, with that fire I want to harness and flame even hotter, to show her all she can be—all they never let her be. Her father has stifled and straight-jacketed her for her entire life.

And then to find her, curled up and nigh unto death in the garden, my beloved labyrinth where I've spent so many hours cultivating my precious roses...

I want to rage. I want to throw things and roar and scream.

But not while I have such precious cargo in my arms. I hold her to me and rub her back as the mud sluices out of her hair, the powerful water cleaning her.

And that's when I notice that it's not just mud swirling

down the drain. There's blood, too. I pull back from her and she lets out a little whine of protest, but I have to see what she's done to herself.

"You're hurt!" Long scratches wind up and down her arms.

She looks down at herself impassively and shrugs. "The rose thorns. It's fine." And then she flashes her big, luminescent green eyes at me. "I don't mind the pain sometimes. My mom used to say that feeling pain meant she was still alive. It's why she loved roses. They always come with thorns. Beauty plus pain. They were *her*."

Then her eyes blink woozily and her forehead collides with my chest again. "I've never told anyone that before."

"That's right, honey. That's good. I'm going to know everything about you. But first, let's get you clean and warm."

She nods into my chest, so much shorter than me that her head only comes up to the bottom of my chin.

My chest squeezes, and not just because she's wrapped her arms around me. I've never— I mean, this isn't what I was— I'm supposed to be the one—

"You'll never be cold again," I lean over and murmur into her hair, and she nods again, like she believes me.

THIRTEEN

Daphne

WHEN I WAKE UP, it's the middle of the night and I'm shivering in spite of the fact that there are blankets piled on top of me.

"Daphne?"

It's him. The Beast. The same one I ran from earlier today. Gods, I'm so *cold*. My teeth are still chattering. I can't remember why I ran. I think he yelled and it all seemed scary? Or maybe I was scared of myself? All the things he's made me feel since coming here?

"S-so c-cold," I manage to get out through clattering teeth.

The fire is blazing in the corner. Even without glasses or contacts, I can make out that much. And when he moves from the chair by the fire, I can see his dark, hulking form moving closer to the bed.

But I'm not afraid. Not now and maybe not ever again. Not of him. Not of the man who brought me in from the cold and so tenderly held me and washed the mud out of my hair. Who tucked me in bed and murmured to me in that deep, rumbling voice of his the entire time. I don't even remember the words he said, just the deep, reassuring bass of it.

A giant, cool hand presses against my forehead and I wince. I'm trying to get warm here, and he touches me with his freezing hand. I pull away.

"You're burning up," he rumbles. Of course I am. My immune system was depressed from stress and no sleep and the stint in the tower, and then a run in the freezing rain...

I frown groggily and peek one eye open at him. Then I squint. I don't even remember closing my eyes. Huh. Funny.

He starts to pull away and walk out of the room.

"No!" I sit up in bed and hold out a hand to stop him, then the room whirls dizzily. I grab my head and wince. Ugh, my head feels full of cotton and I've got a deep, thudding headache.

"Don't go," I still manage to grind out. And then, more plaintively than I'd probably prefer if I were feeling one hundred percent, "Don't leave me alone."

But I feel like crap, so even as I collapse back onto my pillow, I still hold out a wan hand. The scratches on my arm are looking better, the healing salve he rubbed on earlier doing its work. "Please. Stay."

And then I lose the fight to hold up my arm and it drops to the bed, too.

He hesitates a moment in the doorway like he's second-guessing himself but then he comes back to the bed and sits beside me. I nestle against his hip. He radiates warmth.

"You're so warm. Lay down beside me?" I murmur. "I

just need to get warm." A shiver wracks its way down my spine.

"What we need is to get your fever down."

Then he does the last thing my feverish brain expects. He leans down and presses a kiss to my forehead. Every muscle in my body relaxes at the contact of his lips against my overheated skin. It feels so *right*.

He moves to rise again and my hand shoots out, shackling his wrist. And then he kisses my hand. "I'll be right back, beautiful rose. And if you're a good girl and take your medicine, then I'll stay with you through the night."

"In bed with me?" I'm using the last of my energy to hold onto his wrist, but it feels like the most important thing in the world to wrest this promise from him before he goes.

"Maybe so." Another whisper of a kiss to my forehead and then he's gone, and the whole world seems like it's gone cold.

It feels like an hour before he finally returns, but he does come back. With a tall glass of water and a couple of pills.

I try to take the cup, but my strength almost immediately fails me and water sloshes out of the cup and onto my blanket. But he's right there to grab the cup before I drop it completely.

"Here," I've got it, he says calmly. Then he helps me sit up, cradling my back to tilt me up, and he lifts the rim of the glass to my lips.

"Take a sip first," he murmurs, and I do. The water is cool, but it feels good slipping down my throat. When he holds out one pill, I obediently stick out my tongue without waiting for instruction. His lips curve up and I watch the edge of his mask thoughtfully as he places the pills on my tongue and then lifts the glass to my lips again.

This might be the closest I've ever been to him, just able to observe. Everything's still slightly fuzzy through the haze of my fever and with the room lit only by the flickering fire in the fireplace. But still, I can see the fine hairs of his short beard on the half of his face that's exposed, and his lips are full and yet somehow still manly. The skin around his eyes is smooth, young-looking, even though there are shadows there that make me think he's rarely at ease.

I swallow but he doesn't pull back and that's when I realize he's watching me just as carefully as I'm observing him. He lifts a hand and caresses it gently down the side of my face. "What am I going to do with you?" he whispers, but I have the feeling it's more to himself than to me.

"Keep up your end of the bargain," I whisper.

A smile crinkles his lips and he nods. That's all the agreement I need as I slump against him. He's *so* warm and I'm so cold. I've been so cold. I've been cold for so long. Longer than I even realized, I think.

But that's the last thing I manage to think because sitting up and drinking down the pills took more out of me than I expected, and I'm soon drifting back off into the warm cocoon of sleep. Feeling safer than I ever have before in the Beast's arms.

FOURTEEN

Beast

SHE FIGHTS A FEVER FOR DAYS. I pace the floor, cursing myself. I forgot she was so weak, so fragile. Her beauty and brain are so strong, but their vessel is frail. Just like her mother.

I remember her father pacing the floor like this, wearing a tread into the carpet. Finding him in the lab with his head in his hands. He worked night and day for a cure. He never lost hope.

The second I saw her, I knew we were meant to be, he told me once of his wife, Isabella. *With your success, son, you'll have women throwing themselves at you.* He placed a hand on my shoulder. *Take my advice: wait. Wait for the one.*

True love? I'd asked with a jaded smile. He was right; women did throw themselves at me. But only if they couldn't get Adam's attention. He always outshone me. *Don't tell me you believe in soulmates?*

If by soulmates, you mean a woman made for you as you were for her, then yes. Dr. Laurel had been perfectly serious. A scientist who applied reason to everything but his relationship with the love of his life. *True love does exist, son. And it's worth the wait.*

I press my head to the freezing glass, gritting my teeth against the cold. Winter has come with a vengeance. Below, in my rose garden, even the hardiest varieties are bowed under the weight of ice.

Daphne whimpers and I cross the room, kneeling by the bed to take her small hand. I check her forehead. The fever is breaking.

"Stay with me," she whispers through parched lips. "Don't leave."

"I won't, sweetheart." I hold a glass of water to her lips until she drinks. When she's done I ferret out a jar of salve from my lab to smear over her chapped lips. Caring for her feels natural. Like everything in my life led to this moment.

For years I've burned with one purpose: revenge. It's her father's fault that I'm a Beast, too ugly and gruesome for anyone to love. Far from throwing themselves at me—if women ever saw me now, they'd run. Just like Daphne did.

And yet, I forgive her. How can I do anything else when she clings to me so trustingly? My heart was frozen as the winter earth, and her touch melts the bitter frost.

"I'm here, Daphne. I'm not going to leave you."

FIFTEEN

Beauty

"OPEN FOR ME, SWEETHEART."

I glare at the masked man sitting across from me. He regards me steadily. He still hasn't replaced my glasses but in the past few days, the slightly blurred angles and contours of his face, neck and hands have become familiar to me. For all the torment he's dealt, he can be surprisingly gentle.

Even when his patient is increasingly grouchy. And mouthy.

"You know, I'm not a baby. I can feed myself." I cross my arms over my chest.

He says nothing and proffers the soup spoon until it's a millimeter from my lips. I sigh and open my mouth as instructed. *Ugh, broth.*

"Chicken soup? Again?" I settle back on the pillows as he scrapes the bowl for another tepid spoonful. "What I wouldn't give for a cheeseburger."

"You need to replenish your fluids and electrolytes."

"Thank you, Dr. Obvious," I mutter. His good brow raises. I curl my fingers into the blankets to keep from reaching up and touching his face. Not the first time I've had the urge.

He spoon feeds me a few more mouthfuls. Ever since I grew strong enough to sit up, he's insisted on feeding me. I give him a hard time but secretly I love it.

"Don't you have anything better to do than feed me? Tend your roses? Torment another prisoner? Play your giant organ?" I let my gaze flicker to his crotch. Like always, he's dressed impeccably, with well-tailored slacks and dress shirt, shoes and cufflinks polished and gleaming. A veneer of elegance that only draws attention to his powerful body. Always enclosed in such fine clothes, but lately, with nothing else to distract me, I can't deny that sometimes my thoughts wander to wondering what he might look like underneath...

Now both his brows are raised. "My giant organ?"

I blush. "Um, yeah. The instrument, oh Masked One." I flutter my fingers in the air and hum Bach's Toccata and Fugue in D minor. "Like, for composing an opera."

He studies me and I bite my lip, wondering if I've pushed him too far. I've let more of my joking personality out in the last few days, because, fuck it, what do I have to lose? It feels good. I usually keep this side of myself stuffed down. The only one who's seen silly Daphne is Rachel.

"No organ," he says finally, scraping the spoon in the bowl to scoop up the dregs. "No other prisoners. Just you."

"Lucky me."

"Indeed." He feeds me the final bit of soup.

A smile cracks my face. He blinks at the sight of it. I'm as surprised as he is. Here I am, getting nursed back to health by a crazed man in a mask, and I'm almost...happy. I have a million questions swimming around my head—*why do you have a lab? How long have you been studying Battleman's disease? Are you close to a cure?*—but I don't want to break the moment, this temporary truce.

And my instincts are right, because his stiff jaw loosens a moment and the Beast almost, almost *smiles*.

"I'm feeling better. Stronger. Can't I get out of bed?" I've already been up today. He helped me to the bathroom and gave me a bath. Not as torrid as our first bath together, but enough to make me blush.

"Maybe tomorrow." He sets the bowl down and heads over to the fireplace to add a few logs. He keeps the place toasty warm now. There are brocade curtains adorning the giant windows, and thick Persian rugs on the floor. Not that he lets my feet touch the ground. He treats me like a princess. And even though he used to despise me for my supposed addiction to luxury, each day he seems to resent me less and less.

He draws the bed curtains, cocooning me in velvety darkness. His finger ghosts over my cheek before he strokes my hair. "Sleep now."

I catch his hand. He stiffens and I drop it. "Sorry." He never lets me touch him.

A pause. "It's all right."

"Stay with me a bit?"

"And do what?"

It's my turn to stiffen. He's touched me all over, and held me in this very bed, and I know we're headed to something *more,* but I'm still weak and—

"Shhhh, Daphne. It's all right. I'll stay. Right here." He seats himself in his usual chair beside my bed. "Is this what you wanted?"

"Yes. Tell me a story?"

He studies his hands. He often wears gloves but he's left them off to tend to me. The skin is mottled and scarred, as if they sustained chemical burns. "I'm no good at stories."

"Then I'll tell you one."

"You should rest—" he starts, but I grab his hand. He stiffens but I don't let go. I clutch his hand with both of mine, holding on like a lifeline. After a second he relaxes a fraction. Not perfect, but it's a start.

"My mother used to tell me stories. There once was a princess who lived in a castle..." I launch into one of my favorites, a blend of Princess Bride and Rapunzel, with a couple of dragons because why not? "And they all lived happily ever after in their castle surrounded by rose bushes." I finish with a yawn. The Beast hasn't moved a muscle since I took his hand. He might as well be a statue, a dark gargoyle watching from afar.

"That's a lovely story," he rumbles.

"Mmmm," I close my eyes. My grip on his hand loosens. He pulls away, but he takes one of my hands between his, holding it like a little bird. "I like stories," I murmur. "As long as they have a happy ending. My mother said all stories should have happy endings." She felt my childhood was filled with too much pain and sadness.

"And your story, Daphne?" The Beast's voice turns harsh, even as he strokes the back of my hand gently. "Does it have a happy ending?"

"I don't know," I sigh. Sleep's closing in. Even though the Beast is growling again, his big body vibrating tension, I know now he'd never really hurt me. I feel safer with him than I have in a long time. "I guess it's up to you."

MORNING FINDS me curled in a Beast-sized armchair by the fire. Outside a winter storm beats freezing rain against the window, but my body's stronger than it's been in days.

I can't believe the Beast tended me all this time. He's been inordinately gentle. He even let me touch him last night. I held his hand, though I can barely remember our conversation.

The bedroom door creaks and the Beast appears. He sees me and stops in his tracks. "You're awake."

"I got up and dressed all by myself," I brag.

"Well done." There's that glimmer of a smile. I'm addicted to it.

"I brought breakfast." There's a cart with a tray just outside the door. I wrinkle my nose at the shiny silver dome covering the plate. It's probably more broth.

But no, when he whips off the cover with a flourish, a steaming omelet with a side rasher of—

"Bacon!" I reach with both hands, already drooling.

"Ah ah," he holds the plate aloft. "Not until you eat your porridge." He hands me a bowl and spoon. Topped with fresh berries and cream, it's hardly gruel, but it's not bacon.

"You're heartless," I tell him, but dutifully dig in.

"So I've been told." Another glimmer of a smile.

"Careful," I mutter to the bowl. "I'll one star you on Yelp."

"Too late. I've already been voted best Evil Captor three years running." As my mouth drops open—he made a joke!—he adds, "Having a castle helped."

"I bet. How did you get a castle just outside New Olympus anyway? Did you build it?"

"Inherited it. My predecessor brought it over from the old country, stone by stone."

My mouth is hanging open now. The Beast isn't just making jokes, he's sharing information? Before I get too excited, he raises his chin and orders, "Eat, Daphne."

I lift my spoon and plunge it dramatically in the bowl. He watches me take a few bites before kneeling to build up the fire. I can't help but admire the taut line of his backside, set off perfectly by exquisitely tailored pants.

"Remind me to thank your stylist," I murmur.

"What?" he rises, dusting off his hands. Today he's in a chunky off-white knit sweater. His black hair is tousled. Mmmmm.

"Nothing." *Daphne! Stop perving on your captor!* My spoon clinks in the bowl as I shovel away at the oatmeal.

"Careful. Don't make yourself sick."

"I want bacon," I say with my mouthful.

He makes a frustrated noise and kneels beside me, commandeering my spoon. "Slowly," he says, feeding me a smaller bite.

"Fine." I let him feed me as he's done before, exaggerating my movements. "Mmm," I hum and lick cream from my lips. His gaze hones onto my mouth. I nibble on a strawberry and he looks away, jaw clenching. Is that a flush on his swarthy skin?

I sit back, satisfied. I'm not the only one affected.

"Are you finished?" he asks.

To my disappointment, I am. "I'm full," I sigh.

He sets the bowl down and picks up the plate. "Because I'm hungry."

"That was my bacon!" I cry.

"Mine now," he grins outright now, his teeth white and even under his mask. Without the tension in his jaw he looks...handsome?

I flop back in my chair. "One star." I wave a hand at the

grand furnishings, beautiful enough to adorn a modern palace. "Decor is great but the service leaves much to be desired."

"Be nice, now," he admonishes, dragging a second armchair closer before seating himself. "Otherwise I won't share." He holds up a slice of bacon. Gaw, it smells heavenly.

I hold out my hand and he shakes his head. Now I'm flushing. But it's not the first time he's fed me, so I lean in and get my reward. Is there an amused glint in his eyes as he feeds me? Fuck, I don't care. Bacon is the best.

He feeds me all the breakfast meat like that. I wave away a forkful of the omelet, but gleefully accept the tiny cup of thick hot chocolate he serves from a china teapot. With the fire crackling and good food in my belly, I'm as spoiled as a princess from my mother's stories.

When was the last time I had a leisurely breakfast? Without lab reports or quarterly filings to go over? Rachel would be slack-jawed. And not just because I'm enjoying a meal with my evil captor.

By the end of breakfast, it's stopped sleeting. The day is brighter even though the clouds are grey.

"I want to go outside," I tell the Beast.

"It's too cold."

"I can bundle up. Come on, the storm's long over. I want you to show me the gardens." *The labyrinth.* If I don't dare ask him about Battleman's or my company's patents, maybe I can learn more about him.

A ploy, I tell myself. A way to guard myself against my captor. Not because I want to know him as a person. A friend or, gods forbid, a lover.

I mean...sometimes I might have had a few stray fantasies over the past few days, but those don't count, right? I was half-delirious with fever most of the time. I blink away the confusing thoughts when the Beast starts talking again.

"It's winter. They're not at their best." He twists to look out the window. My breath catches at his profile. It's somehow familiar. A memory tickles me...

He turns back, his dark brown eyes catching mine, and the memory is gone.

"We'll have to agree to disagree," I say as he plumps my pillows. "The roses look amazing. My mother would love them."

"Yes, she did love her roses, didn't she?" he murmurs.

How do you know? What do you know about my mother? About me? I bite back the questions.

He puts the plate aside. "It's time for your punishment."

SIXTEEN

Beast

"MY PUNISHMENT? WHAT FOR?" She sits up straighter, pushing back a lock of hair that's fallen over her cheek. Her skin is newly flushed—her healthy glow returned. She doesn't look upset, but curious.

"For running from me."

"Running..." Her forehead creases as if she doesn't remember. Just days ago we were at odds. "Oh, into the labyrinth. I thought you were going to hurt me." She sounds matter-of-fact, unafraid.

"And now?"

She tilts her head to the side, studying me. I hold my breath, waiting for her to recognize me. But she never does. I was too thorough with the details of my disguise. But she murmurs, "I don't think you will. Hurt me, I mean. Not more than I can take." Her lashes lower, fanning across her bright pink cheeks.

Once again I am staggered by her strength. Her willingness to trust. And the way her body responds to me.

Only me.

"Go to the bathroom. Refresh yourself and return to me," I order in a hoarse voice.

Her brow wrinkles for a moment, but she obeys. Just before she disappears into the bathroom I call out. "Oh, and Daphne?"

She turns back, responding instantly to my command. *A good start.* I rise, savoring the moment.

"When you return to me, you need to be naked."

She bites her lip but nods. The bathroom door closes. A few seconds later, the shower turns on.

Ignoring my painfully hard erection, I spin into action. Normally I'd follow and enjoy washing my little captive, but she's going to submit to me. *Willingly.* And I want to be ready.

This is a new step for us. After the labyrinth, things changed. Taking care of her…it wasn't like anything I've ever experienced before in my life.

I've been alone as long as I can remember. It's just been me vs. the world. Alone all growing up, fighting for my place in the group homes and then a series of brutal disappointments as an adult.

I hadn't left the castle for a year before her. I thought it was better that way.

But fuck was I was wrong.

Because when she reached for me in her feverish delirium? When she begged me not to leave her? Her little hands grasping desperately onto whatever part of me she could reach?

I— I just— *Fuck.* I can't even think straight when she's around.

Beyond one clear thought: I need to make her mine.

Right then the bathroom door opens and my heartbeat ratchets up a notch. The lights are dimmed. A few candles and the fireplace add an ambient glow. I've stripped the bed and changed the sheets, leaving off the pillows and blankets.

She's delightfully, deliciously naked. The light from the bathroom limns her smooth curves. Damp tendrils of her hair frame her face. She hesitates in the door, her hands fluttering around her hips as if she wants to cover herself. She doesn't know her own perfection. But then after a moment, her stance firms, her hands fisting at her sides. *My good, brave girl.*

"Come to me." I wait by the bed as she slowly crosses the room. As my shadow stretches over her, her pulse jumps in her throat. She has said she trusts me, but some part of her, the primal instinct, recognizes me as a threat. A predator. *A Beast.*

And I am. I tower over her, big enough to break her in two.

That's why I've waited so long and prepared so much. In my earlier rages, I've risked breaking her which is why I haven't let myself touch her until I was absolutely in control of myself. I need to be gentle as I master her completely. She can never crave any touch but mine.

Her lashes lift, her incredible eyes meeting mine. "What are you going to do to me?"

"I'm going to teach you, sweetness. How to submit to my commands. How to give yourself fully to me."

Her chest rises and falls rapidly. But her gaze doesn't leave mine. I've never had a creature look at me with such trust even as she says, "I don't know if I can do that."

Oh sweetness, you can. "You don't have to do a thing." I can't stop myself from reaching out and touching her hair. My hand is huge next to her face. I grip one of her damp locks, swallowing it in my fist. "Just let go and be mine."

SEVENTEEN

Daphne

THE BEAST LOOMS OVER ME, half in shadow. In the dark, the scarred skin around his mask disappears. When he turns his head I get a sense of deja vu, like I know him from somewhere—

"Go to the bed and lie down, face up."

I swallow. My hands come up automatically to cover my breasts.

"Ah ah," he catches my wrists and moves them apart, baring my chest to his gaze. My heart is pounding, overwhelmed. I'm so vulnerable right now.

Still holding my wrists, he backs me to the bed. When he lets go, I scramble up and lay back. Maybe if I obey him, I won't have to worry. I won't have to think. *Let go and be mine.*

He bends to grab something at the base of the bed. When he rises and I see what he holds, I scuttle to the headboard and plant myself there, my knees drawn up to my chest.

"You want to tie me up?" I squeak. "Again?"

He tosses the chain onto the bed. The silver length has a leather cuff on the end. I clutch my wrist.

His gaze never leaving mine, he heads to the foot of the bed, leans down, and reveals a second restraint. There's one at each corner of the bed. He ends up beside me again, unbuckling the leather cuff for my left wrist.

"Submit, Daphne."

After a deep breath, I do. I could tell myself I have no choice, but it's not true. I could've protested when he announced it was time for my punishment, and he would've backed down, tucked me into bed and coddled me like an invalid. It was my curiosity as much as his depravity spurring us forward. I don't want to stop. I'm in too deep.

I scoot down and lie back. After a pause, I slowly spread my arms and legs. The ultimate submission. That fact that the position makes my pussy throb has nothing to do with it.

"Good girl," he murmurs, taking my left arm and securing the cuff around my wrist. "Flex your fingers for me?" I do and he strokes the tips. His dark eyes bore into mine and my core clenches. He only has to touch my fingertips to turn me on.

"Too tight?" he asks. I shake my head. His cheek curls—another smile!—and he heads down to cuff my feet.

"You're being so good, Daphne. You know what that means?"

"What?" My voice is husky. The sound of it surprises me—I've turned into a sexpot. I've never felt like this before, but this moment is one of many firsts. He's still dressed like always, but this time, I'm unafraid as he strips me bare.

Lying down and letting him restrain me with an excited willingness.

I've never been more turned on. My nipples are crinkled peaks, begging for attention.

"It means you get a reward." He turns and walks away, leaving me helpless and bound. My arms are stretched over my head, my legs able to bend a little but not move much more than that. *What is he going to do to me?*

When he returns, I'm almost panting, my heart fluttering in the cage of my chest like a captured bird. But my nipples are harder than ever. And my pussy aches...

"Shhhh." He lays a large hand on my chest, splayed over my breastbone. "Calm, Daphne. I won't hurt you." A quirk of his lips, a crooked smile. "At least, not more than you like. Because you like some pain, don't you?"

"I...don't know."

He reaches behind his back and I cringe, expecting an implement of torture. When he shows me what he's holding, I almost laugh.

"A rose?" The petals are dark red, just beginning to unfurl.

I crane my neck and he brings the bloom to my face. I inhale the scent. This time memory brings me back to the first time I found the rose—on my pillow in my room at Thornhill. It was a week after my mother died. I was eighteen, almost nineteen. My childhood room felt like it belonged to a stranger, the walls, the bed no longer familiar. Everything had changed. I'd stepped over the threshold from girl to woman, and I would never be the same again.

Deja vu. I'm standing at another threshold now.

The Beast uses the rose to trace the contours of my face. Up one cheek, down the other. Over my lips and down my sternum. He trails the rose between my breasts. The petals tease my already peaked nipples.

"I thought this was punishment?" I manage breathily.

"It is. I'm going to teach you not to be so reckless with what belongs to me." The rose brushes lower, teasing the taut plane below my belly button. When did my skin get so sensitive?

I hold my breath as the rose dips lower.

"One day, Daphne, I will call and you will run to me." It's a promise, a threat, a vow.

I shiver and get that sense of deja vu again. Or maybe a premonition.

He grabs a pillow and slides it under my bottom, propping up my hips. Gods, I'm fully on display now, my labia slick and plump.

"You poor thing. So very needy." He tickles my folds with a forefinger. "Shall your Master make you feel better? Here?"

I whimper.

"Or maybe you want me here." He probes my entrance gently. I clench my thighs, drawing them together as far as they can go. Which isn't very far. The Beast smirks at me, teasing my slick hole as my knees tremble, trying to close to keep him out.

A petal breaks from the rosebud. He rubs the bloom over my folds, tickling my labia. Another petal breaks off, and another. The Beast crouches low and blows over my skin, and I clench my core. The petals scatter.

He spends time with his head angled this way and that, his mouth hovering over me, his lips pursed so each breath sends petals dancing over the bare canvas of my flesh. He sends the petals this way and that until goosebumps rise on my bare midriff and my pussy aches.

Then he straightens, rising over me to observe me like a work of art. My flesh prickles further.

"Beautiful," he finally pronounces, and turns away.

"No," I whimper, tugging at my bonds. I'm aching, dying for him to touch me.

"No?" He shoots a smirk over his shoulder. "Are you trying to tell me something, Daphne? Have I given you any indication that you're in charge?"

I shake my head. Maybe, if I'm a good girl, he'll come back and ease this crazy ache.

He sets a small wooden box on the bed and lays down beside me, his head by my hip. The bed creaks with his weight.

He turns the rose, shows me the stem. The thorns.

"You told me pain makes you feel alive," he reminds me. I raise my chin, refusing to cringe away. He circles my nipple with the sharp point. One wrong move and he'd prick me. My blood would well, the color the same shade as the rose...

"I bought you something."

He sets the rose aside and opens the box, angling it so I don't have to crane my neck too much to see the contents: strangely shaped jewelry adorned with glittering green stones.

"Do you know what these are?" He lifts one to show me the clamp mechanism.

"No," I swallow. "But I can guess."

"I'd tell you," he holds the clamp open over my nipple. "But I'd rather show you." When the clamp closes, the bite sends a shot of sensation straight to my pussy. I breathe out, letting the low-level pain linger and fade away.

The Beast studies my face carefully. He must see the

exact moment when I've adjusted to one clamp, because he nods. "And the other."

This time he holds the clamp open over my nipple for an interminable moment. I have to close my eyes. My focus makes the bite worse, or maybe it's just the compound pricking sensation from two clamped nipples.

"Beautiful," he says again. "Open your eyes, Daphne."

I obey and he teases the undersides of my breasts with the rose. My breasts feel fuller, aching not with pain but with need.

"These are far from the most intense clamps I could use. You look so lovely, I might find a pair you can wear all day. With emeralds to match your eyes."

"You're nuts," I say without heat.

"Careful. I have a third clamp I could use."

Third clamp? "Where..." My voice trails off as I realize what he's threatening. "Oh." My eyes widen. "You'd clamp me...there?"

"I would. I will. Not today. We'll work up to it."

I should be mad, raging at the thought of him adorning my breasts and clit with jewels and parading me around his castle naked, but I'm panting, incomparably turned on.

"I wonder," he murmurs, with a studied glance at my pussy. "You can take the pain. But do you like it?"

He rises from the bed, repositioning himself between my legs. With my hips elevated, I can only see the dark top of his head as he bows over me. I stifle a moan as he nuzzles me.

"Oh, Daphne, you like it. You like it very much." He raises his head enough for me to see his evil expression. "You know what this means?"

"No," I gasp, my chest heaving.

"There's so much for us to explore. So many combinations of pain and pleasure. So many ways to make you feel alive..." He lowers himself down and I let my head fall back. I can't fight anymore. When his tongue finally touches me, I give in.

EIGHTEEN

Beast

SHE TASTES SWEET. I've scented her before but this is my first taste and oh *fuck*. I'm supposed to be the one in control here. I fist my fingers into the sheets, chasing her honey with my tongue. I need more. I need every drop. Her lithe body jerks, the emeralds winking at me.

My erection hardens to stone at the sight. She's submitted so beautifully. Without qualm or question. Only trust. Trust in *me*.

No one's ever given themselves to me so freely, *before* or certainly not after I was scarred. No one's trusted me like this in my whole life. And for it to be *her*, Daphne, my Daphne—

The time of punishment is over. Now I'll reward her so well. I'll play her body and make it sing.

I undo the nipple clamp even as I suckle harder on her clit. Her head flies back, her body shaking in the grip of orgasm. Her cries ring out.

That's right. That's right, beautiful.

And just when her cries reach their crescendo, I undo the second clamp and the second rush of pain hits her, prolonging her orgasm or launching her into a second, I'm not quite sure. But I'm there, just the tip of my tongue flipping ruthlessly back and forth over her clit until she's screaming at the top of her lungs and thrashing on the bed.

Pain plus pleasure just delivered her the most incredible, raw climax of her life. Unbelievable.

She stretches out her hand as far as the restraints allow, moaning, "Please. Please let me touch you now."

I lift my head from between her legs, my own erection pulsing so hard it's painful between my legs. Sweat dots her brow and her hair is damp against her forehead. Her pupils are blown from pleasure.

She's the most beautiful fucking thing I've ever seen in my whole fucking life. I can't stand it. I have to have my own relief.

I want to thrust inside her beautiful, dripping sex. Even imagining her tight heat enveloping me is almost enough to have me spilling in my pants.

Daphne, *my Daphne*, finally, I could finally—

Instead, I whip away from her and yank my cock out of my pants, grab the base of it and then pump furiously.

Daphne

HE TURNS FROM ME. His head bowed, his shoulders hunched and shuddering. He's jerking himself off and no matter how I crane my head, I can't see anything beyond his dark profile, gilt in dying firelight.

He's still completely dressed while I'm stretched out bare and naked. Even now, while he pleasures himself. I can somewhat understand about his face, but why does he hide the rest of his body from me?

And he won't let me touch him. Why? Does he hate me that much? Or is he ashamed of how he looks? The thought strikes me and I sag back. I don't understand, there's so much I don't understand.

The Beast groans. His back judders as if he's cumming. For a moment there's no sound but his ragged breaths.

Then he heads to the bathroom—I still can't see anything. When he returns, the side of his face I can see is unreadable, but he has a warm cloth in his hand and a jar.

He sits on the bed beside me, silent at first as he rubs the warm cloth between my legs. When he finally speaks, a wave of relief runs through my body. "You were beautiful tonight. I'm so proud of you."

Why do his words make me want to cry? After all I've achieved in my life...but as he dips his fingers into the jar of what turns out to be salve and rubs them oh so gently over my poor, abused nipples, I realize that all the praise I got throughout my life was never about me. I was always praised for what I achieved. Not for who I was—at least, not after my mother died. Tears spring to my eyes and I blink them back, hoping he doesn't notice them.

Next he undoes the restraints, rubbing the marks on my wrists. So gentle now, the opposite of the demanding Master earlier. Or maybe not the opposite, maybe it's just the other side of the coin. This is the whole man. He'll never inflict more than I can handle, and he'll always be here after to soothe and care for me.

I curl into him as he gathers me into his arms and carries me to the armchair. I'm drowsy. Where I was strung tight as a guitar string earlier, now I'm limp and loose.

He builds up the fire and returns to the chair, lifting me and taking a seat. I'm in his *lap*, surrounded by his warmth, his strength. He's still dressed and I'm still naked, but it's still so good, so wonderful to be so close to him. I've never felt more connected to a human being and I never want him to let me go. He's touching me everywhere, and in my way, I'm touching him. Well, the most he'll let me.

I don't know how long we sit like that, cozy as a couple. I try to stay awake. I don't want to miss a moment...

But it's...so warm...so...cozy...

My eyelids droop.

I fall fast asleep.

WHEN I WAKE UP, I'm curled up in the same chair, but I'm alone, a blanket settled over me and while the fire is still going, it's dying down. And the Beast is nowhere to be found.

I sit up and look around in confusion, scrubbing at my eyes.

I tug on a long sweater and slippers and go in search of him.

As soon as I start heading down the main staircase, I smell something amazing.

I still don't know my way around the castle, but I follow my nose.

Gods, what *is* that? It smells *so* freaking good and just now do I realize how freaking hungry I am. It's only today that I've really gotten my appetite all the way back after being sick and I feel like I could eat a large pack animal.

The main floor of the castle is beautifully decorated. I only glimpsed it during my mad dash through the place when I ran out into the labyrinth. But now as I go, I take in the antique furniture, some of which looks almost a hundred years old.

I can't imagine the Beast hunting antique stores to find all this stuff or hiring an interior designer to fill the castle.

But right, he said he inherited the castle from his 'predecessor', whatever that means. That word makes is sound like whoever it was wasn't family, but why else would someone give away a *castle* in their will to just one man?

It's one mystery after another with the Beast.

I press my hands to my face and pause by the windowed double-doors to the back garden. My whole life has been upended by a man I know literally nothing about. It's insane. Completely and utterly nuts.

So why does it feel like at the same time I feel closer to him than anyone else in my life? That he knows *me* better than anyone ever has before?

The sun is setting, the castle casting long shadows over the huge labyrinth garden in the back, purple and electric pinks spilling across the sky.

I press my hand to the cold glass. You never get views like this in the city. And when was the last time I paused to watch the sunset? To notice anything beautiful?

"There you are."

I startle, but only a little, as I turn and see the Beast standing at the other side of the expansive sitting room.

"I was just coming to get you. Dinner's ready."

His eyes move from me to my hand on the glass of the

double doors. The same ones I fled through. Does he wonder if I was thinking about running again?

I step back. "I wasn't going to—"

"I know. Come. The food will get cold."

Just hearing his calm, confident voice sends a thrilled little shiver down my spine. Gods, he's electrifying.

I didn't know that just being with another person could make me feel like this—like I was a dormant robot out of battery and then he came along and plugged me in. But even as the thought hits me, I bite my lip. That's not quite true. I felt like this one time before, but it was a long, long time ago and I gave up on ever having it again. Or anyone ever wanting me back in the same way.

I glance up at the Beast as he leads me towards what I assume is the kitchen or dining room. *Does* he feel the same way as me? Why is he doing all this? Why does he have the Battleman's research downstairs? Is he— Does he actually feel something for me or is this still all about my dad and Adam?

It all *feels* so real.

But I suddenly feel sick to my stomach and almost lose my appetite thinking that this all might just still be about revenge. That I'm just a pawn to him, naïve and foolishly giving my heart when he doesn't—

"You're quiet. That usually means you're coming up with a thousand disaster scenarios to worry about."

I freeze and stare at him. How does he know that about me?

He chuckles. "Stop worrying for once and let's enjoy dinner. You must be hungry after all our exertions earlier." He lifts his good eyebrow and smirks at me, then pushes through a door and leads me into the kitchen.

Gods it sends butterflies flittering through my stomach

every time he's flirty like that. And look, the kitchen is on the first floor after all.

I glance briefly around at all the modern appliances that have been installed, though the overall feel of the décor is still castle-chic. It's really a beautiful blend of modern and antique, burnished stainless steel appliances amid stonework.

There's a small wooden table with plush chairs off to the side of the kitchen, a cozy little space to eat by a large bay window.

The Beast puts his large, warm hand to the small of my back and leads me towards the table, already set with plates heaping with food.

"Shrimp broccoli stir-fry."

"It looks and smells amazing." And it does. Being in his presence, his hand on my back, suddenly my appetite has come back full force. When I'm with him, all my doubts and worries disappear. Foolish maybe. Definitely.

But there's just something about him. I can't explain it. It's the farthest thing from logical, when usually logic is what I pride myself on.

The pull to him is undeniable, though.

And when he pulls my chair around so that we're sitting thigh to thigh, I love it. Every touch thrills me. Settles me.

I want to sink into him and never look back. Nobody warned me it could be like this. I'm helpless to his magnetism.

Maybe he sees it in my eyes because he reaches out and runs his hand up my back to my neck. He settles his hand there and massages slightly at the same time he takes a forkful of shrimp, broccoli and rice and lifts it up to my mouth.

My bottom lip trembles as I open to him. It feels luxuriant and naughty to let him feed me. It was one thing while I was sick in bed.

But here, both of us sitting at the table, it's— It's—

"Lick the fork clean," he murmurs, the pressure on my neck intensifying just the slightest bit, sending a shiver through my entire body. Shit, how is him feeding me so hot?

I nod and run my tongue along the tines of the fork before finally, sensuously releasing the fork and chewing my bite.

His dark eyes flare and then he takes a bite of his food from the same fork. A simple act but one that feels ridiculously intimate.

We repeat this little dance for several more bites until I'm all but squirming in my chair.

Okay, screw dinner. I want him to shove the plates to the floor and for him to put that sinful mouth on me.

Even the memory of earlier has me wet.

Which reminds me...

"I'm not wearing anything under this sweater," I suddenly blurt. Then I lick my lips and lean in towards him. "And I'm probably making a wet spot on your nice chair."

If I thought his nostrils flared earlier, it's nothing to the way his pupils darken and his nose huffs out like a bull.

"I don't know whether to take you across my lap or praise you for being a *very* good girl."

His hand stays on my neck while the other, which he'd been feeding us with, drops the fork and immediately reaches beneath the hem of my sweater. And goes straight to my sex, where he dips his finger right in.

He hums in satisfaction when he finds me as wet as I promised and his finger slips in with ease. He pushes in up to the first knuckle. Then the second.

I squirm in my seat and drop my legs open to give him

easier access. I don't even really mean to do it, it's becoming a reflex. He touches and I respond. I never imagined being mastered could feel so— so—

"*Ohhhh*," I moan and he smiles and his finger pulls out of me with a slick, slippery noise.

"Enjoy your garnish, my sweet," he says, then he lifts the finger he just had inside me, glistening with my own wetness and paints my lips before slowly, oh so slowly, shoving his huge, manly finger in my mouth.

"Now suck."

He tilts my head with the hand at the back of my neck, manipulating me like a doll while I suck his finger, and I suck it fervently, needing to break through his calm demeaner, needing to drive him as crazy as he's driving me. Needing to know I affect him.

And finally, finally, he breaks and pulls his finger from my lips and then his mouth is on mine.

Kissing me.

My *first kiss*.

And it's the most erotic freaking thing ever, him tasting my sex on my lips.

I'm inexpert. I don't know what to do, how to kiss him back, but I try. Still, he must sense something is a little off because he pulls back, confusion in his eyes. "Daphne?"

I feel my cheeks flame and duck my head. "Is it that obvious I haven't done it before?"

He suddenly grabs my face with both hands and forces me to look him in the eyes. "Are you seriously telling me that was your first kiss?"

I blink and try to look down again but he won't let me. "Tell me the truth," he demands.

"I— I mean, I just never— I never had a boyfriend or

anything." Is he really going to make me explain this? "I just work. That's all I do."

His jaw clenches so tight I think it might shatter but he manages to get out, "What about Archer?"

"It wasn't— I mean, he'd just told me he wanted more at the ball, but before that we'd always just been friends and—"

His lips are on mine before I can say another word.

And *oh*, kissing. Kissing is marvelous. In spite of his dominant nature, he doesn't just shove his tongue down my throat.

He teases. He teases like a proper devil, dancing along the tip of my own tongue in a way that lights up every single nerve ending in my whole freaking body.

He breaks away only long enough to murmur, "You sweet, innocent girl. You've let me debauch you in so many ways when you hadn't even ever been properly kissed?"

He kisses me again, sweet and soft, his hands creeping into my hair. Finally, long minutes later, he presses his forehead to mine. "You're impossible. You shouldn't be real."

I giggle at that. "Of course I'm real. And I have to say, kissing is *amazing*."

He growls low in his throat. "Let's rephrase that. Kissing *me* is amazing."

I laugh again, so fucking happy. He only wants me kissing him? Fine with me. "As long as it's a two-way street, buddy. Kissing *me* better be the only amazing kissing you're doing, too."

He pulls back and looks at me like I'm an alien. "You're definitely not real." He shakes his head. "Now eat up."

He puts another forkful of food to my lips.

I obey, all the kissing having excited me more than ever.

I'm more than curious to see what he might have in store for us after dinner.

But when I'm full and can't eat anymore, he grabs my hand and doesn't lead me up the main staircase.

Instead, we head to the servant's stairs that head *down*.

NINETEEN

Beast

SHE'D NEVER BEEN FUCKING kissed.

I have claimed all of her firsts.

She's mine completely.

But when she finds out all my secrets? When she finally sees beneath the mask? What then?

I'm not proud of the abject fear that clenches my chest at the thought. I clasp her hand as we head downstairs simply because I need the contact with her skin. *Me*, wanting human contact. That alone should tell me how fucked sideways I am.

We arrive downstairs and I don't turn on the lights. I know this place so well that navigating in the dark past my gym equipment is easy. I could flip the switch…but I want her trust. Need her trust.

And she doesn't balk but only holds tighter to my hand as I lead her forward. The small demonstration of her faith in me makes my balls tighten.

She's so trusting.

But she's never trusted anyone else with her kiss or with her body.

I want to press her against the wall right here and thrust inside her, bury myself so deep that I don't know where I end and she begins.

But no, I can't. Not when I've only just found out how very innocent she is.

Soon. Soon, but not right now.

She deserves the smallest slice of normal. She never had a childhood. And now I know there were no first dates, no fumbles with boys in the dark...

I have to bite back a growl even at the thought but I just give her hand a slight squeeze as I lead her forward.

I can give her everything she never had.

Starting with a first date.

I flip on the lights and she curls into me, blinking against the light. Every time she does that, naturally turns into me, fuck, but it kills me.

When she finally realizes where we are, her eyebrows scrunch in confusion but she also smiles up at me. "Bowling?"

"Bowling."

She laughs, still looking confused.

"You ever been?"

She shakes her head.

Of course she hasn't. Did she ever take a day off in her life from studying and working to ever do anything fun, just for herself? I can already guess the answer is no. Her bastard father forced her to grow up isolated and when she got old enough to be useful, he drained her dry. She was only ever a thing to be used. She's as much his victim as I am, she just doesn't see it yet.

My hand squeezes into a fist before I force myself to relax it.

"Come on," I urge her over to the rack of balls.

"They're all huge," she says, hurrying over with her hands clasped together and eyes bright. She's excited and I fucking love seeing it. "I'm not sure I'll even be able to pick it up."

"That's why I had a Daphne-sized ball delivered yesterday."

I pick up a small, deep purple ball on the bottom. The finger holes are so small I don't even think the tips of my fingers would fit inside, but Daphne takes it delightedly and her delicate fingers slip inside with no problem.

Her bright eyes come up to mine. "It's a perfect fit." She gives a hesitant half-swing. "And it's not too heavy for me." She beams up at me.

So fucking trusting and easy to please.

I can't help drawing her close in spite of her bowling ball smushed between our stomachs and kissing her. Her lips are just as soft and plush as before, but less wooden as she learns how to kiss back.

Her first day ever having been kissed. The thrill of it still goes straight to my cock and I'm glad for the bowling ball separating us so she can't feel how hard I am. I'm going to keep this a PG date, godsdammit.

So I pull away with one long, last lingering kiss. When I finally pull away, her pupils are blown and she looks absolutely dazed.

From a fucking kiss. Killing me. Fucking *killing* me.

"First the shoes."

I pull out two pairs from the low drawer underneath the bowling ball rack. Also in yesterday's delivery. There's a fresh pair of socks for her. She steps out of her slippers and sits daintily on the bench to put them on beside me as I do the same.

But then she stands up and heads towards the single lane, and it hits me all over again that she's not wearing any pants. Not even any fucking underwear.

She's a virgin vixen.

I want to punish her. I want to please her. But most of all, I'm determined to give her tonight.

"How do I throw it?" She takes a terrible first experimental swing that would have sent the bowling ball flying into the wall had she actually let it go.

"Not like that," I chuckle, walking the short space between us and lining myself up behind her. My cock is very conscious of her bare bottom only inches away. But if I'm to master her, I can certainly master myself.

It doesn't mean I won't remind her of what's between us.

So I lean over from behind, my breath in her ear. "Start by standing like this." I straighten her up so she's facing the pins. "And hold the ball like this, nice and loose and ready to release."

I reach around to help her rearrange the ball and her breath hitches. I smile and stroke her wrist with my thumb as I pull back.

"Good. Just like that," I murmur, my breath making the hair by her ear flutter. And yes, I do enjoy the shiver I feel go down her spine in response.

"Now what?" she asks, her voice slightly breathy.

"Well, you're right-handed, so you step with this leg," I slide my hand down from her waist to her left hip until my hand is settled on the outside of her left thigh. "And then swing with this arm."

My arm braced behind hers, together we take a practice swing. "And see those little arrows on the lane down there?"

I point to the marks on the floor and she nods. "Those are guides. If you aim for the fourth one over, you can get a strike. Going for the one in the middle will give you a split."

She nods, biting her bottom look, looking adorably concentrated. "I wanna try."

"Go ahead, baby."

I step back and sit on the bench. "Remember to face the pins. If your body is tilted even the littlest bit, that's the way the ball is going to go when you release it."

She turns and makes a face at me. "I got it, Mr. Know It All."

I smirk and gesture for her to continue. She gives several practice swings before finally releasing the ball. It rolls about two feet before landing in the gutter and moving slowly, *very* slowly down the lane.

Daphne stomps her foot. "I want to go again. That wasn't— I just lost my grip before I was ready!"

"Of course you did, baby," I humor her. "Don't worry. The ball's coming right back."

I had a new mechanism installed when I inherited the place so her ball returns up the shoot quickly and she's up again, glaring down the lane. She does make an attempt to square up her body parallel to the pins, but at the last second she twists diagonally and the ball ends up right back in the gutter.

She throws her hands up and spins around, the hem of her sweater lifting to reveal a tantalizing amount of thigh.

She notices me looking and her annoyed expression fades. She comes towards me, the vixen expression back in her eyes. "Why don't we do something more entertaining?" She tries to climb in my lap.

I laugh and grab her by the waist, depositing her on the bench beside me. "When was the last time you tried something you weren't naturally good at the first time? No, no, this is quite entertaining enough. Plus, it's my turn now." I nip her on the lips and then pull back.

I grab my favorite ball and head towards the lane. I've spent more hours than I'd ever admit down here on endless lonely nights. I know the quirks of this lane and when I wind up and release, the ball flies out of my hand and down the lane. It explodes into the pins and they're all knocked over.

Daphne jumps up and claps. "You got a— What do they call it? A knockdown?"

Fuck, she cracks me up. "A strike, baby. They call it a strike."

She grins at me as she comes over, holding her ball to her stomach. "Okay, I wanna learn. I'll be a good girl and listen."

Does she know what those words do to me? I'm *very* tempted to toss away the bowling balls and take her up on her earlier offer, but the light sparkling in her eyes is too much to turn away from. Fun is a foreign concept to her, so I tell my dick to shut the hell up and together we go back to the lane.

The machine has reset all the pins and she lines up again, doing several experimental swings that would definitely have ended up as gutter balls if she'd let them loose.

We spend the next thirty minutes working on her form and she gets that familiar expression on her face like when she's studying a hard problem she has to solve.

And when the first ball goes straight enough to actually *make* it all the way down the lane and actually strikes some pins, she whoops so loud and starts jumping up and down, I grin wider than I ever have maybe in my whole damn life.

This woman. This fucking woman.

I grab her up in my arms and kiss her. She swings her arms around my neck, which makes me immediately tense up but then her lips are on mine. Her cheek is mashed against the leather of my mask, but it's like it's not even there for her, she's so eager to get at my mouth. As if I'm a whole man to her.

Gods, I want to devour her. And as much as I've been patient, she's thrusting her groin against mine, lifting a leg to wrap around my ass to pull me into her...

But she's touching me. Touching... She could feel, or if she—

I finally growl and grab her wrists, yanking them away from around my back. She's startled and breathless and her leg drops.

Then I grab her around the waist and carry her the two feet to a smooth wood-paneled wall and thrust her up against it just like I dreamed of doing when we first walked in the room.

I hold her wrists above her head and kiss her and she keens underneath me, that one leg again coming up to snake around my thigh and urge me into her.

Who the hell was I kidding? Things can never just be PG between us.

I lift the bottom of her sweater and whip it off over her head.

Exposing her perfect, beautiful body and nipples so hard I have to have them in my mouth this fucking second.

I suckle her left nipple into my mouth even as my hand traces the same curves I caressed earlier. Down her hip to her outer thigh, but this time I massage around to her ass. So plump and round in my hand. It reminds me of how this sweet little ass peeked out at me every time she bent over to throw the ball.

I give a quick swat but that only makes her thrust her groin against mine again, seeking friction. It's a good move because there's certainly friction to be found, I'm so hard in my pants, I'm like a heat-seeking missile, solid and pointed straight towards her warm, slick pussy.

I know she's slick because after I squeeze her luscious ass, I tease a finger between her thighs and she's absolutely drenched for me. Dripping down her leg, even.

All I want is to open my pants and thrust inside her. To impale her against the wall and fill her with my cum. To mark her from the inside out as mine.

My cock pulses against her with the need. It would be so easy…and she wants it, if her whimpering, hip thrusting, and little breathy pleas are any indication.

But there's so much she doesn't— Can I really, when she still doesn't even know—

Frustration bubbles over at my own indecision until I bark, "Down on your hands and knees."

She pauses, definitely seeming startled by my sudden u-turn, but she's a quick study because as soon as I let go of her wrists, she bends to the floor and takes position, so beautifully obedient, her peach-shaped ass upturned towards me.

I'll reward her so good. So, so good.

I immediately get down on the floor behind her. "You're doing so well. You handle everything I throw at you. You're beautiful. Fucking perfect."

I brace one hand beside hers as I bend over her and bow my forehead to her spine, between her shoulder blades and trace my other hand over her plump breasts and down her stomach to the heated heaven between her legs.

I lift my head just enough to whisper in her ear, "Do you want to feel me?" I nudge my still-clothed cock against her sweet ass. "The real me?"

"Yes," she all but chokes out. "Please, oh, please. I want to feel you."

There wasn't an ounce of hesitation in that answer so I reach down and give us both what we've been wanting.

I release myself from my pants and my long, hard cock finally gets to meet her sweet flesh. I play with her pussy as I press my length between her ass cheeks.

She arches her back, thrusting her ass back up against me. "Gods, you feel amazing," she breathes out. "Please. Put it inside me. I want it."

My cock pulses again, so close to her dripping pussy. But *I* am in control here and have already decided how this will go down…even if it was a deviation from my original plan. Like she does with everything, Daphne screws with my equilibrium in a way like no one else before her.

But in this, at least, I'm holding on to the last scraps of my sanity, and mainly because her naked body is beneath me and my fat cock is stretched between the most gorgeous ass cheeks on the gods' green earth. Never have I felt more like master and commander of my own destiny and also on the edge of completely losing my entire self—will, soul, and mind—to the tiny woman beneath me.

Paradox. That's her.

But she's my fucking paradox to tame, like trapping a whirlwind.

I smack at her pussy lightly. "Remember who your master is," I chide lightly, before slipping first one finger and then a second inside her, stretching her, at the same time strumming her clit with my thumb.

That silences her, apart from a series of pleasured moans and squeaks. I finally give in to my own desires and thrust myself up and down the natural channel made by her round ass cheeks.

So fucking beautiful. So fucking hot.

I need more. I need so much more. This is torture, knowing her pussy is so close. But sadism comes with the territory when you've been made a monster, so it's nothing new. And even the barest touch of her soft, perfect skin... She bucks so enthusiastically back against me as I rile her up, closer and closer towards her own orgasm.

Her pitches rise in pitch.

"That's right. That's right. Ride my hand. I'm fucking your ass cheeks and it's so damn hot. You have ass cheeks any man would fucking die for."

Her cries reach a scream as my words take her over the edge. I lie on top of her so that my cock is sandwiched between our bodies and I fuck her ass cheeks even more fervently. I curve my fingers back in a come-hither gesture, teasing at her g-spot even as my thumb keeps at her clit.

She thrusts back into me like a bucking bronco, a wild animal in the height of her pleasure. I jack my hips forward as my spine lights up, my balls tighten, and—

I cum so fucking hard that I own the entire fucking universe, everything I ever, *ever* fucking wanted complete in this moment, clutching this beautiful woman to my body and sharing the apex of pleasure with her.

But even as the world blinks back in, I know—this is only the beginning. If it felt *that* good to cum outside her, what would it be like to be face to face, that pussy that's clenching like a vice around my fingers sucking the cum from my cock, her lips on my lips, looking into her eyes as we draw the pleasure from each other and share it—

But would we really be sharing it if she doesn't even know the real me?

Can it ever be anything more than a mirage, like the mask I wear?

I bow my forehead to her spine again, not willing to lose this moment just yet. If I clutch her to me tight enough, she'll never leave, right?

I release her right then.

Because that's not a man's logic, it's a boy's. The point of all of this was to make her crave *me* and be unable to live without *me*.

So why do I feel like *she's* the one who's mastering me instead?

TWENTY

Daphne

I BLINK my eyes lazily awake. I'm still in the Beast's arms. He's running his fingers through my hair. I lick my lips. I couldn't have been asleep more than half an hour.

We have a habit of falling asleep like this for naps in the afternoon. In front of the fire, me curled into his big, warm body. Usually after some sort of festivity that leaves me naked, and him still clothed, like always. But both of us well-sated.

I don't move even though I'm awake, wanting to hold onto the moment for a little while longer. Today over lunch, he stripped me and set me on the table, feasting on *me* instead of lunch before our afternoon nap. Gods, he makes my body absolutely electric, and after I cum, I turn into a limp rag, liquid in his arms, and become quickly sleepy. I'd always heard it was guys who fall asleep after sex but I swear I've never found a more effective sleep aid.

The last few days have been...indescribable. When I'm

with him, everything else disappears. Our 'date' last night was so sweet, him teaching me how to bowl. Then it turned so hot, feeling him skin to skin against me.

I've never in my whole life let go like this. Taken a time out from the world and...and...done, well, anything like this. I mean, I never even took vacation days! And now to hide up here like at a spa—the Beast certainly likes giving me hot baths often enough—and to experience so much *pleasure*...

My cheeks spike with heat just thinking about all the things we've done together. Which reminds me of the one big thing we *haven't* done.

I'm still a virgin.

He holds back. For some reason I can't understand and he won't explain. Then again, he's not big on explanations, is he?

Whenever I *do* stop and think about it, I start freaking out a little—he seems to know everything about me, but what do I know about him? I want to know everything. I want to understand. I want to feel like he's in this as deep as I am.

But how long can I continue investing myself...investing my *heart*, without answers? We're becoming so close. Surely it's time. I just want to *understand*.

And he's in a good mood. He's cum. I've cum.

It's now or never.

"We've never talked about what I found in the basement that day."

He jerks back, his eyes flashing a warning, but I forge on. "What are you doing down there? Why are you working on Battleman's? Why did you really buy the patents from my father?"

His nostrils flare. He pushes me off his lap. "On your knees."

He's so frustrating! "Why can't you just be honest with me? Haven't I earned that? I've given you everything. Trusted you with *everything*. My body. My spirit." I pound my chest with my fist. "With my *soul*."

"On. Your. Knees." He points a meaty finger towards the floor.

I drop to my knees in front of him, but I don't bow my head. I stare up at him defiantly.

"What will it take?" I shake my head, beseeching as a terrible thought strikes me. "Or was it never about that? It doesn't matter how much I change or open up? You never meant to do the same. To bend for me or meet me in the middle."

I choke out the next words. "You only ever meant to break me and then leave me that way."

He lets out a roar that echoes off the stone walls. "No! Never!"

And then, to my shock, he pushes the chair back and drops down to *his* knees, right in front of me and his hands are on my face and his lips are on my lips. They aren't gentle. They aren't kind.

His lips crush mine. Begging. Punishing.

For once, for *once*, my hands aren't tied down. And I want to tear off that fucking mask he uses to keep as the last barrier between us. I want to, so badly.

But I've just been telling him he can trust me. So I won't prove otherwise the first chance I get. Instead, I wrap my arms around his neck, so close to the elastic tie of his mask but not touching it. His breath catches. Does he realize? Does he *finally* realize all I have given and would give for him?

His hands are on my wrists the next second like always, though, clasping them both in his huge grip. In one swift motion, he flips us so that I'm on my back on the sumptuous rug, the fire burning bright and warm beside us.

My naked nipples pebble in the chill air even as the warmth from the flames dances over my skin. My back arches into his touch as he runs a hand down between the valley of my breasts and my sex clenches in anticipation.

"Let me see *you*," I gasp, wriggling to get free of his grasp. Because while he let me feel him yesterday, he was zipped up before I could even look over my shoulder at him. He never lets me see anything, know anything about him. And I can't stand it anymore. I need something from him. I need him to give an inch even if I really want a mile.

A rumbling growl of dissent starts in his throat but I shake my head. "Just your clothes, I mean. I want to see you." What he'll let me see, anyway. But I'm starting to hope this is a process, in spite of what I said a few minutes ago. Maybe because I'm just fooling myself?

Or maybe because I hope, in spite of himself, he *has* bent for me. I'm not sure what he intended when he first brought me here, but from the vulnerability I now glimpse in his eyes, I suspect this isn't it.

He's been so tender and caring. And commanding and dominant. Obviously, there's been plenty of that, too.

But even now as he hovers over me, my hands held solidly in place, his strong thigh between mine in a way that drives me crazy, I've never felt more free. He's introduced me to myself these past days. I was only living half a life and I couldn't even *see* it. It was a rude awakening, that was for damn sure, but would I go back to being asleep?

Especially when being awake means I get to be with *him*?

No. Not for anything in the world.

"I want to see you," I say more quietly, even as I wriggle against his thigh.

He cracks a small smile. "You want to see my body?"

"Gods, *yes*." It's all but a groan as he tweaks my raw right nipple, and then the left. They're still so tender but the memory of earlier and the brief twinge of pain has my sex lighting right back up again.

He arches an eyebrow. "Only good girls get treats. Can you leave your hands where they are? One twitch and this little experiment ends."

I nod fervently. "I promise. I won't move an inch."

He caresses a hand down and teases between the lips of my sex, and then he circles my clit with his glistening fingertip. I arch so violently at the first spike of pleasure. He immediately pulls his hand away and waves his finger in my face. "Ah ah ah, don't make promises you can't keep."

I can smell my own scent on his hand, and even after all we've done together, I still feel my cheeks burn hot. But I immediately drop back down to the rug and lift my hands back over my head. I look him in the eye. "I won't touch you. I give you my word."

A small furrow appears between his eyebrows and he hesitates another second, but then he pulls off his suit jacket and his hands move back to his collar. He begins to deftly undo the buttons of his crisp white shirt.

I can't help licking my lips. *Finally*, after all this time I'll get to see what's beneath the hyper-polished facade. Surely his muscles won't actually be as big as I've imagined them, not in real life. Back in the beginning I hoped he was wearing some sort of padding underneath the suit so he'd appear larger than he actually was.

But as he slowly peels off his shirt, and then grabs the

back of his undershirt and yanks it off over his head—holy *shit*.

The man is a Greek god.

He's a statue made flesh.

How— Just *how*? How is this god-man a recluse who lives out in the middle of nowhere? Where are all the sycophants who belong on their knees at his feet? Yes, I suspect his face is injured somehow, he's obviously endured some sort of terrible tragedy, but *still*—

"You're gorgeous," I whisper. And I want to break my promise so badly. I want to reach out and touch his huge, muscled chest. I want to press my hand over his heart. I want to kiss down his torso and— My eyes travel the line of hair from his belly button into his pants.

He's watching my every reaction and his six-pack flexes in response to my shameless gaze. My calves flex and my toes point in anticipated pleasure.

"More," I whisper, then swallow. When did my throat suddenly get so dry? "Please, I want to finally see what a man looks like. What *you* look like."

Is it just my imagination or are his hands shaking the smallest bit as he drops them to the button of his bulging pants?

I bite down on my bottom lip as he unzips. I swear a zipper has never moved so slowly before in the history of all zippers. I gasp as he finally reveals himself.

He's gigantic *down there* just like he is everywhere else. I swallow and look away before almost immediately glancing back.

"Look your fill," he says in a low, masculine rumble. "Look, but remember, don't touch."

I nod rapidly and blink. The more I look, the more *it* seems to grow, even though I wouldn't have thought that was possible. I'm rapt as he leans up and tugs his pants down the rest of the way and then kicks them off, along with his socks.

Okay, now the whole god look is complete. He looks as amazing and perfectly muscled as any statuary in the most world-class museums.

"You're the most incredible thing I've ever seen."

I only notice his scowl when he snaps, "No more talking."

I look back up at his face. There are a hundred questions on the tip of my tongue. Why is he like this? Why does he hide his face behind a mask? Doesn't he understand that there's more to life than looks? Yes, I certainly appreciate his beautiful body, but I've become fascinated by him *in spite* of his scary hulking size and the mask he hides himself behind. We've connected in ways I never knew were possible and I've never even seen his *face*. Doesn't that tell him everything he needs to know?

"One last question?" I chance.

He glowers at me but I risk it. "Will you show me how you touch it?"

This question at least doesn't seem to anger him, though. And I can't help licking my lips again as his huge, powerful hand grasps the base of the large, veined shaft and strokes it roughly up and down.

"Doesn't that hurt it?" I gasp.

He shakes his head. "So innocent. Didn't you ever watch videos? Online? Or look at pictures at least?"

I suck in a quick breath as I continue to watch him stroking himself. His eyes are locked on me. His inspiration seems to come from watching my reaction to him.

"I always kept SafeSearch on," I whisper breathlessly.

"Of course you did," he murmurs. "My little virgin. But

you like looking at my cock, don't you. You can barely take your eyes off it."

I look up from his pulsing member to meet his eyes. "I think I was waiting for you even though I didn't know it."

He groans and lets go of himself, reaching for me in the same moment and crushing his lips to mine. "Good answer," he growls between punishing, demanding kisses. If I'm not careful, he'll swallow me whole.

And I just might let him.

He's back over top of me, but finally it's not the rasp of smooth, Italian fabric against my skin. It's him. Hot skin against skin.

He might not let me touch him with my hands, but so much of the rest of us is touching. And I can feel him there against my thigh, hot, hard, and pulsing. His *cock*. A pulse of heat clenches in my stomach and then shoots down between my legs. I bite down on his tongue in my mouth, I can't help it.

But that seems to drive him even crazier. One of his hands tangles in my hair and the other slides down my waist and then around to my ass, first cupping, then squeezing, then slapping my ass. My hands are still above my head and I writhe in his arms.

"Harder," I gasp out my dirtiest desires because he is my safe place. Nothing is off limit, nothing is wrong here. While I can't use my hands, at the same time, I'm unleashed.

And he obliges. Oh hell, but he obliges. He slaps my ass and the sharp sting of pain while he continues to devour my mouth makes all my pleasure centers light up. I focus on the sting, the way it ripples outwards like a pebble in a pond to the rest of my body and then lingers as heat on my skin.

And then, because he always knows what I need before

I can even think to ask, he spanks me again, even more sharply. I cry out and bury my head in the crook of his neck, my hands fisting above my head and my hips thrusting blindly towards his.

It's so thrilling to have this much contact with his body, so much more than he's ever allowed before. If all I have to do is keep my arms above my head, I'll show him I can obey the rules. This is heaven. Better than heaven. Where will he take us next? Will we finally— Will he explore me with more than his fingers?

Gods, I want it with every fiber of my being. I don't want to be a virgin anymore. But only if I'm with him. I want him to make me a woman. *His* woman.

I want us bound together in every way. I want to feel him inside me. I want to surround him with my womanly softness and let him bury himself deep. He's been my safe place and I'll show him I can be his. And eventually he'll learn he doesn't have to hide any single part of himself, not anything—

I open my eyes and breathe in the manly scent of him, my cheek pressed against his firm chest. I'm so close that for once, my near-sightedness isn't a hindrance and I admire the expanse of his skin, the hair that dusts his pecs, the constellation of freckles on his shoulder...

Wait.

WHAT?

I jerk away from him and scramble so I can sit up. Then my hands shoot out and I grab his arm and pull him closer—well, I move myself closer to him—I probably couldn't move him if there were three of me.

Closer examination proves what can't possibly be true. But it is.

I know this constellation of freckles. I know it well. One

summer, me and this shoulder and the man attached to it became very, very familiar.

"What the fuck?" I ask just as he yanks his arm out of my grasp, eyes flashing angrily. "You promised not to touch me."

He's already pulling his shirt back on but I know what I've seen. And there's no going back.

"Logan?" I ask, my voice breaking on the two syllables. "Logan, where have you been all these years?"

TWENTY-ONE

Logan

"LOGAN," she cries the name I haven't heard spoken aloud in so long, and certainly not from her lips. It's been years.

And then, before I can seize control of the situation again, she reaches forward and yanks the mask off my face. Her touch sears me as the mask falls away. Not because it hurts. I lost feeling in most of that side of my face a long time ago. But it still stings when she gasps and her hand goes up to her mouth in shock.

"Logan, what happened?" Her eyes fill with tears.

This is the part where most people run. I know just how hideous my face looks. The skin from my forehead to my chin on the left side is a mottled spiderweb of angry, red, vein-like scars. My left eye barely survived. My ear didn't.

Flesh-eating bacteria will do that to a man.

I broke all the mirrors in my apartment when the 'accident' first happened. Ha. *Accident*.

The flood of memories brings all the barely-buried rage

back to the surface and I snatch Daphne's wrist out of the air when she reaches forward like she wants to touch my face, to touch the freakshow science experiment I've become.

"Don't," I snap, not letting go of her wrist. Her tears spill down her cheeks.

"What happened? You just disappeared. I looked for you but you weren't online. Your emails bounced back undelivered. I went to your apartment but you were gone. I couldn't find you anywhere. I thought— Dad said you—"

"Tell me," I sneer. "Where did the great Dr. Laurel say I'd gone? What lie did he tell you?"

Confusion colors her face. "What do you mean? I don't understand."

"He did this to me!" I roar.

She immediately starts shaking her head, looking horrified again for the second time in as many minutes. "No, Logan, you can't believe that! Dad would never— What even happened? Is it a burn of some kind? Or—"

"Bacterial infection. The rare flesh-eating kind."

Her mouth drops open.

"A strain so rare the doctors said they had no earthly idea how I could have contracted it. Except that Belladonna labs had a research sample in-house at the time."

"Well then it must have been an accidental cross-contamination. One of the lab techs didn't follow proper safety procedures or—"

"Stop being willingly obtuse," I shout, letting go of her and spinning away, giving her my back. "Your father and Adam wanted me out of the company. They'd stolen my research and had already colluded to profit off of it. They just needed me out of the way."

Is she still going to keep defending them even with the

evidence right in front of her? Of course she will. I'm a fool if I think the past few days have made any difference at all.

"Logan. Nothing you're saying makes any sense to me. What are you even talking about? What research?"

"*I* was the one who discovered the anti-aging capabilities of the molecule we were developing. Adam said we should explore the commercial possibilities in cosmetics as a money-making opportunity. All he saw was dollar signs. I said no, that we couldn't get distracted from our core mission of focusing on curing Battleman's and other rare diseases."

I stare at the wall, unable to keep the bitterness out of my voice as I continue. "I thought your father agreed with me. He did, to my face."

I turn and look at Daphne. She's so perfect, her naked body shaped with the same care the gods must have taken when they shaped the first woman. It hurts to look at her and remember what her own father did to me. "But behind my back..." I shake my head as my teeth clench.

"How do you know any of what you suspect is true? Can't it just be a horrible coincidence that the company was transitioning at the same time a terrible accident happened to you and—"

"Don't be so naive." I slam my palm against the wall and she flinches. I'm scaring her. How quickly I become the Beast again to her. But there was no hope of me being anything else now that she's seen my face, was there? I was a fool to entertain any other idea, even for a moment. Especially considering I'm dealing with *his* daughter.

"He and Adam were in on it together. Adam made sure I had an open wound for the virus to enter through. On my *face* no less. He's one grisly fuck. To want to infect someone's face with a flesh-eating bacteria," I laugh darkly, "that takes a truly twisted mind. Though to this day I don't know if it was the brainchild of Adam or your dad."

"Stop it," Daphne cries. "My dad would never do that!"

"Then how do you explain the fact that when the city's Disease Control investigators looked into it, they discovered the source of infection was my lab goggles? Your father and Adam spread the bacteria on the *exact* spot where Adam had split my cheek open in a fight the night before. Are you going to call that coincidence? Please continue to astound me with your naiveté."

She glares at me but then I can tell my words sink in. "That still doesn't mean—"

I scoff. "How about the fact that Adam had his father pay off said Disease Control investigator so that said lab report never saw the light of day? And I was shuffled off to a private hospital where no one knew where I was. The infection became so bad when I was in the ICU I coded twice. I *died*. Do you understand? They succeeded. They killed me."

"Oh my—" She comes forward at this and tries to reach for me but I block her hands with my forearm and glare at her.

"Don't. Touch. Me."

More tears glaze her eyes. "Oh, Logan. I had no idea. I should have been there. I *would* have been there. It kills me that I wasn't there when you needed me."

Her eyes move back up to the ruined half of my face but she doesn't wince this time and she doesn't look at me with pity, either. Her eyes are full of...of some sort of feeling. She's looking at me with a familiarity beyond that of just submission or the excitement I've seen her exhibit in our sexual discovery during our time together.

She's looking at me like...like she knows me. She's

looking at me just like she used to. But she can't be. Not now when I'm a—

I shake away the thoughts and turn away from her again. I can't bear to have her eyes on me anymore. It's too much, too soon. Especially when she still thinks her father and her precious Adam are innocent. I know she does.

She wants to believe everyone in the world is good.

But at least now I finally know she *is* as innocent as I think I always secretly hoped she was, even if I lost all my own naiveté long ago and told myself *no one* is innocent. I think maybe I've stumbled across the one person in the city, maybe the whole fucking world, who still is.

The same innocence that allowed her to open to me like a blossoming flower is what keeps her from being able to believe her father and Adam are the monsters I know them to be.

It stings, no it fucking hurts like an ax to the chest that now that I've finally told her the truth, she doesn't believe me. That her loyalty to them is so steadfast.

But she hasn't turned away from me either. Not even when faced with...my *face*.

"Logan," she starts but I shake my head in one decisive *no*.

The time for words is done.

"Come with me." I reach out my hand. It's true I've been a bastard. I've locked her away in a tower and chased her through the labyrinth. I've scared her and thrilled her and showed her parts of herself she never even knew existed. And now I've revealed myself to her. Her old friend, deformed inside and out.

But now I give her a choice. A proffered hand. To take or leave.

Will the girl of my dreams take it? Her perfect bronzed

skin glows in the firelight. The princess who was always far too good for me even before I became the Beast lurking under the bed in the stories.

But Daphne, being Daphne, clasps my hand almost the moment I extend it.

I don't give her a chance to second-guess herself. I wrap my fingers around hers, engulfing her small hand in my huge one, and head for the stairs.

I sweep up the stairs, only slowing when Daphne calls out, "wait, Be— I mean, Logan, I can't go as fast as you. My legs aren't as long."

I slow down but my impatience is bristling. I won't believe she truly means it until— I shake my head. I just need to reestablish a sense of order. For both our sakes.

I take her to the one place she's never been.

My bedroom.

It's pitch black inside and I release her hand, not flipping on the light but walking over to the lamp on the nightstand. I click it on and the room is cast in dim light.

"Why are the curtains drawn?" she asks, coming in and turning around slowly.

"No more questions," I bristle. She's looking at all my things as if hunting for clues. She won't find many. My room is all but bare. There are some books on my nightstand. My laptop on the desk in the corner.

She opens her mouth like she's going to ask another question anyway but I beat her to the punch. "On the bed."

For a second, she just stands there before me, the perfect specimen of woman.

But more than that, she is my Daphne. The beautiful girl I watched blossom into a woman before my eyes back when I was a post doc student working for her father. I didn't notice her much until she turned eighteen. There was a dance—a *ball*, I guess those pretentious fucks call it. But she was there and suddenly Dr. Laurel's kid daughter was all grown up, glowing and gorgeous and all *woman*. She's only grown more beautiful over the years, but even back then, she was heart stopping.

Afterwards, I'd come across her in the study carrels of the lab, head bent over, glasses slipping down her nose as she poured over the latest research reports, determined to help her father save her mom. She was always alone. Her father certainly had no time for her, other than for her help with his research.

She gave and gave and gave, taking care of herself and her father and slavishly devoting herself to research. But who took care of her? She asked nothing for herself. She'd spent her whole life in service of others. And as far as I can see, she's still living the same way, slavishly taking care of her selfish father and his company with no thought to her own needs or wants.

Not anymore.

"Logan," her eyes are full of that same intense emotion I saw in her eyes earlier, but more. There's desire. The desire, at least, I've come to recognize. And then come her words, "Logan, I want to touch you. I want to touch you everywhere."

But I'm already shaking my head. A man can only be pushed so far before he breaks. Can't she understand that? I don't say another word. But I will remind her that she is mine. That this changes nothing. That I won't allow it to change anything.

So instead, I walk to my bedside table again, open the drawer, and remove a sleeping mask. I prepared the room, planning for this moment, even if I never imagined it playing out this way.

I walk slowly back over to her, my back straightening with every step. Yes. This is who I am now. In command.

I am the Master here. And she is the object of my desire, who I will pleasure beyond the heights of imagination. I will claim her completely and eventually, her loyalty will be to me alone.

I cover her mouth with a finger when she opens it again. *Silence.* And with my other hand, I slip the mask on over her head, and finally, finally, over those searching eyes of hers that see far too much.

A wave of calm sweeps over me as soon as her eyes are covered. She can no longer see the monster.

I am only the Master now.

TWENTY-TWO

Daphne

HE TAKES my hand and leads me forward. The mask is annoyingly thick. I can't see a thing. But I...I trust Logan.

Logan.

I still can't believe it. How could it be *Logan*, after all these years? And the terrible story he told me. His face. What he believes Dad and Adam did— I have to set him straight. Dad could never— And Adam, he's—

My leg bumps into something soft and Logan commands in the Beast's voice, "On the bed."

I immediately start to climb on the bed, already conditioned to obey that voice. But it's Logan! Logan was always so soft-spoken and gentle. I don't know how to reconcile the two in my head.

"On your back." I obey. Just like every time I've given in while under this roof, it feels so shockingly *good* to give in and follow directions without fighting or weighing every pro and con a million times like I always have to do in the outside world.

I know that wherever the Be— Wherever *Logan* will take me will be amazing. Gods, it's been Logan this whole time. *Logan* who touched my body. *Logan* who touched me down *there*. Who touched *inside* of me. Who watched me come undone and scream out in pleasure. Oh my gods. My face flushes so hot I think my skin might burn off.

But just as I go to cover my face with my hands, Logan snatches my wrists and lifts my hands over my head.

"That's right, my kitten," he murmurs, sounding like a confusing mix of Logan and the Beast, skimming his hand up my forearms to my wrists and quickly and efficiently shackling the soft, padded wrist cuffs on.

It's cold in the room without a fire going and chill bumps rise all over my skin.

Logan makes a *tut tut tut* noise. "Don't worry, I'll warm you up soon, kitten." His hand skims down my body, blazing a path of heat as it goes. Just like always, my body lights up at his touch.

"Just this once, I'll give you a choice," his warm breath comes at my ear. He's on the bed with me, I felt the dip of the mattress as he climbed on and his warmth at my side.

He shifts my body to the side and slaps my ass, giving me the delicious sting that I love. "Do you want me to take you to the space where you can zone out and lose yourself in the pain and pleasure? Do you want to float away and entrust yourself to my capable hands? I'll take care of you. You know that I will, precious."

He soothes the sting he just caused, rubbing in the warmth on my ass where he just smacked.

"Or," he whispered, his voice taking on a deeper growl, "do you want to continue what we started downstairs. Do you want to explore what a man feels like? What *I* feel like, inside you." A thrilled shiver runs down my spine, only rocking me deeper when he continues. "But mark me, once you feel me inside you, there's no going back."

His voice goes darker still. "Once I claim you, you're *mine*. There will never be another man for you. I tried to deny it for years, but you've always been mine, Daphne."

Everything he's saying is overwhelming and I want it. I want it all so badly, I didn't even know how badly until it was offered on a platter by this delicious, damaged man. There are still so many unanswered questions, so many things I need to know.

But there's only one thing I need to know before I give him this answer.

"Tell me this—am I *yours*? If I- If I say yes," my voice trembles, "If I say yes, will *I* be the only one for *you*, too?"

A low groan is all the response I get before his lips crash onto mine. And then I'm not cold anymore, because his body is covering me.

"Little fool," he finally pulls back long enough to say, "I was always yours."

He was always—? Wait, does he mean—?

But before I can question it any further, his commanding lips are on mine again. I still marvel at the amazingness that is kissing him. His soft, plump lips. The expert, exquisite play of his tongue against mine. But then he's gone again, nipping at my lips with his teeth. But then his tongue is back at its devilish work, at the same time his hand tracks down my body to my breast.

It's even more tortuous with the mask on because I have absolutely no idea where he'll strike next. I'm helpless before him with my hands strung up above my head, spread out before him like a feast. And oh, how he feasts.

His mouth breaks away from mine and I whine, but it's cut off by a sharp gasp when his hot lips sucker on to my left nipple, suckling and then nipping again with those damnable teeth of his. My back arches and I cry out at the same time a wave of wet heat gushes from my sex. Oh thank goodness he didn't tie down my ankles. Twisting and writhing my legs together is the only relief I can find because he's straddling my stomach when all I need is something for friction *between* my legs.

Although I can't deny that feeling his smooth, velvety hardness against my stomach isn't also a huge turn-on. Again I hate the blindfold. I want to look at it more. I want to touch it. My face flames, but gods, I want to— I want to *lick* it. I want to do every wicked thing to Logan's body.

Logan! Holy shit, it's Logan on top of me. It hits me all over again and I squirm even harder as a new wave of heat hits.

How many afternoons did I daydream about what it would be like to kiss Logan Wulfe? I had such a huge crush on him. It was the one indulgence I allowed myself. I thought it was harmless because there was no way he could like me back—dorky, nobody little me. No boys ever liked me like that. I was too bookish, far too nerdy, not pretty like the other girls who knew how to do their hair or what to wear, and I never knew what to talk about. I never knew what movies were popular or what was on TV.

But Logan, he was one person I could actually *talk* to. And he was *so* handsome. Girls liked him. They liked both him and Adam. But Logan spent time with me. We'd talk for hours sometimes in the lab while we waited for lab results. I was so much younger than him, I knew he probably thought of me as a dorky kid sister, just nineteen while he was in his late twenties.

But now to find out he liked me, too. *Liked me*, liked me.

And now he has his hands on my—

He slips a hand down between my thighs and—

My back arches off the bed and I cum hard. Fucking hard. Logan. *Logan.* Oh fuck, this is *Logan*. Logan wants me. Logan called me *his*. He said no one else could have me.

The orgasm keeps going and he rolls my clit. "That's right, baby, keep calling my name."

Oh shit, was I saying all that out loud? But screw it. I'm finally with Logan. Logan's about to be my first.

"Logan," I scream even louder, lifting my legs up to get as much contact with his body as I can. "Please, please," I'm begging even before the orgasm comes all the way down. "Please, Logan. I want it all. I want you inside me. Please, I dreamed about this. I want to be with you. I want you to do it. To make me yours. Please, Logan."

"Oh fuck, Daphne." He presses his forehead to my breasts. "You don't know what you're asking." I hear the vulnerability in his voice, the dominant man sounding suddenly conflicted. "I'm not sure if this is right, if you know what—"

Damn him. "I know what I want. Don't tell me I don't know what I want." He's stripped me bare in so many more ways than one. So for once in my life, I'm going to ask for exactly what I want. "I want you to fuck me. Please fuck me with your huge cock. I want you—"

"Oh," I cry out as he shifts and impales me.

"Like this," he breathes out, voice dark. All I can do is nod and focus on all the foreign sensations flooding my body and mind.

"Your sweet little cunt is gripping me like a vise," he hisses, "and I'm barely an inch inside."

There's more to go? This isn't it?

Maybe panic flashed on my face or something because he's immediately soothing. "Shh, you're all right baby. You can take me. Let yourself go. Give yourself over to me." His voice deepens with command. "Stop thinking. Give the thinking over to me."

I nod fervently. Yes, that's what I want right now. I want him but I don't want to have to make decisions. I'm so tired of making decisions. I want him to lead and I want to follow because *oh*, I know it's so good to follow where he can take me.

"That's good," he croons, shifting his hips and pressing relentlessly further inside me. I cry out in surprise at the invasion, widening my legs and cradling them around his hips. Finally, a touch he'll allow. I wrap my legs around him and lock my ankles around his back.

As if this drives him crazy, he grunts low and his hips piston forward, shoving the last several inches in. My chest arches up at the intrusion, thrusting our chests together, my hard, pebbled nipples rubbing against the bristling hairs that dust his chest.

"You're inside me," I whisper in amazement. "Logan, you're inside me."

"The first and the last," he says darkly before grabbing my face and crushing his lips to mine. And then, like he has to imprint his words on my body like a solemn vow that needs a ceremony to seal them, he begins to piston in and out of me.

I don't know how to describe it. It's uncomfortable at first but not exactly painful. He's so *large*. I cherish it. I've never felt more feminine. But not delicate. He's not treating me like some little delicate piece of glass to put up on a shelf for fear of breaking.

No, I'm a woman now. Raw. A woman to be *fucked*. And that's what he's doing. He's fucking me and...and making love to me at the same time, I think. Or maybe I'm over-romanticizing it. Maybe I'm—

"I must not be fucking you hard enough if your brain is still working so hard in there," he says low. "I guess I'll need to do more to distract you."

Oh, shit. "No, Logan, I'm here with you, I swear. This is just all so—"

But he's already pulling that amazing log between his legs out of me. I clench at the loss and feel like crying. No, I didn't mean to ruin it. *Please*, I want to beg, I'll do better next time.

Logan only flips me over on the bed, though. "Hands and knees."

"Are you going to...punish me?" I ask, breathless. I think back to the spankings he's given me here and there. The playtime with the roses and thorns. Do I want this to be that? But then I remember. I finally remember and my whole body relaxes.

I've given up the decision making. Oh thank the heavens. It's all too exhausting. How have I even kept it up all these years?

Logan must feel the wave of relief in me and know what it means because he immediately slides a hand down my shank, rubbing my ass sweetly before landing a sharp smack, then soothing the hot sting with his hand. "That's my good girl. Give yourself over to me. No more thinking. For this little while, turn off that beautiful mind of yours."

Then he leans over me from behind and his breath is hot on my ear, causing wisps of hair to tuft with each word. "I take that back. You're allowed to think about two things and only these two things. You may think of me. And you may think of your pleasure. But that is all. Am I understood?"

I nod.

"Out loud."

"Yes."

"Yes, what?"

"Yes, sir."

Another smack of my ass. "Good girl."

And he's right there, hard and hot and thick at my entrance again. I gasp as he shoves back in with no preamble. As if, now that he's taken my virginity, he can just take me whenever he wants. Now that I'm his by rights.

Oh gods, why does that thought thrill me? Him. I'm allowed to think about him. So I do. I imagine him on his knees behind me, his hands grasping my hips for leverage as he thrusts in and out. I bet his ass looks spectacular, muscular and powerful as he thrusts in—*oh*, he's going deeper than ever. I didn't know he could go so deep. Did he just nudge my cervix that time?

I thrash on the bed and bury my face in the pillow but Logan's not having that. He puts his hand at my throat and pulls me back up. "No. Straight up on all fours."

The gesture is so commanding and he leaves his hand there on my neck, long, thick fingers applying the slightest pressure at my pulse point. Holding my life in his hands.

My hips buck back against his length that's impaling me. I've never— I didn't even know it could be like this. On TV and in the movies, the few I've seen, they never—

"Ohhh," I cry out as Logan shifts his angle of entry slightly and hits the most amazing spot inside me.

"Yes, that's right," he says, his voice more growling and guttural than I've ever heard it. "I will fuck and defile you and you will love every fucking second of it."

"Yes, sir," I say, clenching around him and bucking back with all my inexpert enthusiasm. Oh, oh, it feels so good, better with every filthy word that comes out of his mouth. I'm not pure here. I'm not perfect. I can be dirty and *real* and pornographic and celebrate every messy, glorious moment of being fucked.

He shifts his hand from my throat so that his thumb is in front of my mouth. "Suck it. Suck it like you want to suck my cock."

Even though his cock is impaled inside me, it's his words and suggestions that trigger a fresh flood of wetness. I eagerly suck his thumb into my mouth and he starts to thrust into me even more fervently.

"Yes, *yes,*" he hisses out through his teeth like he's barely managing to contain himself. *I'm* doing that to him. *I'm* driving him crazy like that. It's insane and only sends me higher. Especially when he demands. "Harder. Suck it like you fucking mean it!"

I clamp down on his thumb and pull on it as hard as I can with my mouth and my tongue, creating a vacuum.

"Yes, like that. Fuck, your pussy's just as tight as that. This tight little virgin pussy that you saved just for me. For your true Master. I'm going to reward you for that. I'm going to take you so many places."

He plucks his thumb from my mouth. I whine as soon as he's gone. I want him back. I want his filthy, possessive words back.

But I didn't need to worry. Especially since I should have known that he's not done shocking me tonight. Far from it.

The finger I just lubricated for him? Suddenly that same finger is probing...*at my backside.*

"Logan!" I call out sharply.

There's a brief pause, and then, in a low, dangerous voice, "Do you not trust me?"

Crap. I suck in a deep breath. "Yes. I trust you."

"Good." A smack to my bottom, first my left cheek, then my right.

Then that thumb is back probing at my most forbidden place. My eyelashes flutter underneath the mask. I've never — I mean, *obviously* I've never— Who on earth would think about touching back *there*, like, *sexually*?

Logan's voice echoes in my head, reminding me of my extreme naiveté. This is obviously something people do. Something *Logan* does.

I take another deep breath and then I- I sway my ass ever so slightly back against his touch. I trust him. If this is another new place he wants to take me, I- I want to go. I trust him, and everywhere he's led me so far has been to extreme pleasure and self-discovery.

But he's a horrible tease. He's slowed his pace in and out of me with that huge, beautiful instrument of his, lazily fucking me now and his finger teases at my back hole. It's not just the thumb. I can't see, obviously, but I heard a small *snick* like a bottle being open, and then his fingers are slippery as they circle my hole.

"Forbidden little cherry," he murmurs. "I won't take you here tonight. But one day, and soon. I will take every virginity you have to offer. There is nothing of yours that won't be mine, you understand."

When I'm silent too long, he prods me, thrusting forward with his hips.

"Yes, sir," I yelp as he hits that place inside me that makes bright light erupt behind my eyes. I'm left breathless for a moment. Dear— Was that an orgasm? Did he just carelessly give me a toss-off orgasm? Did he know he was doing it? Then I roll my eyes behind the eye mask. Logan does everything with precision and he knows how to play the female body like an expert harpist.

His fingers circle and play at the entrance before he pries my cheeks apart. My face flames in embarrassment. How can he be so fascinated with...*that* part of me. Or is it not about his fascination at all, but simply the fact that he knows it makes me so uncomfortable and he revels in pushing my boundaries? He loves bringing us right here... where I'm forced to crack open a place inside myself I've always kept closed. Literally and figuratively.

He wants all of me.

Nothing held back.

And I want it, too. Gods but I want it, too. So, turning off the part of my brain shouting that this is a place that should *not* be touched, was never meant to be touched by another person—

Instead I embrace the strangeness of the feeling and lean my ass back into his probing fingers and I relax all of my muscles back there. I let him *in*.

And his greedy fingers take what I give, one thick digit slipping inside and making me gasp as he makes it past the initial ring of muscles.

"Such a good girl," he croons as he explores my ass. Such a foreign feeling, all the while his cock pumps in and out of me, filling me up. And just when I think I'm so full to bursting—with him, with all the sensations that are building in my body—another finger probes at my ass, wanting to squeeze in beside the first.

"I can't," I whimper. "It's too much."

"I tell you when it's too much," he says. "And you can take more." The heat in his dark voice has me clenching around his length.

Yes. Yes, I want to take whatever he has to give me. So I nod, but his biting voice is there the next instant. "Out loud."

"Yes, sir. I'll take what you give."

He spanks my ass and I yelp, then my back arches in pleasure. And then his finger is back, as relentless as ever.

He plunges his cock so far inside me, I feel him all the way to my womb, so hot and hard inside me. I clench around him. It's the best feeling in the universe, being stuffed full of him. How did I live before knowing what this felt like? Before knowing *him*. Knowing him like *this*. This intimacy of bodies and mouths and tongues—he kisses and bites down my spine like he's ravenous for me.

Logan. *My* Logan.

I want to clutch him to my chest. Bury my fingers in his hair. Attach my mouth to his and never let him escape.

But he has his rules so I hold him tight the only way I can, clenching, unclenching, then squeezing again as tight as I can around his cock and fingers. I want to pleasure him as intensely as he's— Oh oh— He's hitting that spot and it's so— It's so—

I cry out my pleasure wantonly, praying I'm driving him even half as crazy as he is me.

When I finally start to hear him swear, losing control, my pleasure soars higher. It's working. He's right here with me.

"Fuck, so tight. Daphne, everything I ever—"

He doesn't finish the thought but his thrusts become even more reckless. "Gotta fuck you. Have to be so." He punctuates his words with a ruthless thrust. "Deep." Thrust. "Inside you." He bottoms out, but that's not enough for him apparently.

He pulls the fingers out of my ass so he can grab my hips to start pumping even more furiously.

"Yes," I cry. "Logan, yes, just like that. Right there." On his every inward punch, he's hitting that spot that lights me up.

Then, at the last moment when he's more frantic than ever, he reaches around the opposite hand that was inside me and begins to stroke at my clit.

"Cum, now," he orders haggardly, "I command it."

And just like that, fireworks explode outward from my stomach, looping down to my sex and then spasming outward to my whole body.

"Logan," I scream, and I keep screaming it until my voice is all but gone, I'm limp on the mattress, and Logan, *my Logan*, is curled on the bed behind me, one strong arm wrapped protectively around my waist so that I'm snuggled into him.

Daphne

I WAKE to the scent of roses. Eyes closed, I smile and stretch my arms above my head.

"Good morning, beautiful," a voice rumbles above me.

I open my eyes to find blue ones staring into mine. "Logan," I whisper. "It wasn't a dream."

"No." He leans back, giving me room to sit up.

"Your eyes..." I frown in confusion.

"Are still blue. I wore contacts."

I sit up. "I knew I knew you somehow. I kept getting flashes of deja vu!"

He chuckles. "Here." He gently sets something on my face. "This will help you see better."

I touch the familiar frames. "My glasses!"

"I knew you'd eventually uncover the truth. Part of me wanted you to." He looks almost shy. Vulnerable. The Logan I knew.

I throw my arms around him, practically tackling him. He chuckles and helps me climb into his lap.

"I know you." I gaze into his beautiful eyes. "I will always know you."

"No one knows you like I know you," he says, and a bell tolls, deep within my soul.

"You told me that before. Years ago."

"It's still true."

I repeat now what I told him then. "My father and mother still loved me. They wanted what's best for me."

"Your mother, certainly. But your father..." Logan shook his head. "He was blind to everything he had."

"He loved my mother."

"Love can blind as much as ambition."

"Hmm." We'll see about that. In the soft morning light, him with his blue eyes and me in my glasses, I'm seeing more clearly than I ever have. My gaze strays beyond the bed and I gasp.

My room is filled with roses. Vases and vases full of them, on every surface. Petals sprinkled on the carpet, around the chairs, on the bed.

"Roses," I breath.

"Happy birthday, Daphne. I'm a bit late this year, but..."

"It was you," I whisper, staring at the room. "You were the one who left the roses. On the day of the funeral, and every anniversary since."

"I knew you were grieving your mother. But I also wanted to celebrate you."

"You mean, the rose wasn't for my mother?" The world tilts. "It was for me?"

He nods. "Your father and I had fallen out by then, but I couldn't stay away completely. The day they buried your mother—"

"Was my birthday. You remembered my birthday," I murmur to myself. "You were the only one." My father was mindless in his grief and Adam had Archer Industries to run."

"I'll never forget the promises we made each other." He turns sober. "I waited for you, this year, at her grave. We promised we'd meet there one day."

"I forgot. Logan, I thought you were gone forever. They told me..."

He sits up straighter, his expression hardening. "Yes?"

"It doesn't matter," I mumble, staring at my hands. "I don't want to talk about *them*." My father and Adam both lied to me about Logan. What else have they lied about?

His big hand closes over mine. "I'm here now. And I'm not going anywhere."

I meet his eyes, that clear ice blue. "I would've come to the grave if I'd known you were there. Logan, I would've run to you."

He swallows. "Even though I look like this?"

"Yes. I don't care how you look. It's you." I cover his scarred cheek with my palm. "It's always been you."

After a moment, he clears his throat. "I know today isn't actually your birthday. You were so sick, I wanted to make sure you were feeling well enough for—"

"For what?" I interrupt, eager for a Logan-sized surprise.

"Patience, kitten," he gives me a mock stern glance.

I giggle, but inwardly shiver. *Logan the Dom. So sexy.*

"I have another gift for you. If you're feeling up to it."

Squee! "Why wouldn't I be up to it?"

A sexy frown. "I was rough with you last night."

Just like that, my bottom remembers how sore it is. I shift a little, but can't stop my grin. "Worth it."

He looks about two seconds away from making me bend over for inspection, so I add, "I'm fine. Really." I cover his hand in mine. I'm wet at the thought of inspection, but I want my present more.

"Very well," he sighs, and produces a blindfold from his pocket.

I cling to him as he carries me down several flights of stairs. The castle no longer feels drafty. "It must cost a mint to heat this place," I say out loud.

He chuckles. "Worth it. I never want you to feel cold. Now," he sets me down. "Stay right here. No peeking."

He leaves me shimmying with excitement, dancing in place. The light hits my face and I turn towards it. I shimmy more vigorously.

"You're too cute," he murmurs, coming behind me and undoing the blindfold. "Ready?"

He whips the cloth away, revealing a narrow room with floor to ceiling shelves. Full of books, of course.

"A library!" I twirl slowly. So many books. "You can't give me an entire library."

Logan chuckles softly. "Can't I?"

I grin at him over my shoulder, and keep exploring. At the end of the room, a fire crackles, surrounded by heavy leather armchairs. Perfect for a winter's night in.

"Logan, this is too much."

"Then I'll wait to show you the rest of your gifts."

"Like what?" I'm being shameless but I can't help it.

Fortunately, he thinks it's cute. "I was going to let you have the lab, too."

I press my hands to my mouth. "Logan…" I shake my head. "It's too much."

"You're worth it. This is what I always wanted to give you, Daphne. This is why we had to wait."

"How did you get this castle, anyway? You said you inherited it from your predecessor. But did you actually find your family?"

He turns, hands in pockets "No. Not my family. My mother was poor, as you know."

"I know. I'm sorry. I thought you might have…found your father."

"No. After I nursed myself back to health, I looked for a new partner. A successful businessman reached out to me, actually, desperate for someone to help. He had an autoimmune disease similar to Battleman's. I tried some experimental treatments and extended his life by several years."

"So he gave you a castle."

Logan shrugs. "His wife had died a decade earlier and they had no heirs. He brought me on as a partner in his business, I helped expand it—"

With the help of my father's patents, I almost say, but bite my tongue. We've come so far in the past few days. I don't want to break the spell just yet.

"—One thing led to another and…" he shrugs again. "Castle."

"Just like that."

My dry tone makes him grin. "Just like that. Do you doubt me, kitten?"

"No." I retreat until my back hits the shelf. He looms

over me, one arm over my head, so he can cage me against the bookshelf.

"I just...we didn't have to wait. I know you wanted to... prove yourself or whatever," I flap my hand, my voice faltering as his eyes glint. "but you were it for me. It was always you." I twine my hand in his thick black hair and tug his face closer.

"Daphne," he groans against my lips, and then we're kissing. He lifts me, propping my hips against the shelves. *Holy hell, Imma about to get hot and heavy in a library...*

My stomach growls, though, ruining the moment.

With a curse, Logan sets me down. "I need to feed you."

"I'm all right."

"You're still recovering," he says in his no nonsense *my will is law* voice. "I forget myself around you."

I bite my lip to hide my smile. If I can make him forget himself, can he forgive the past?

I SNEAK a smile at Logan over my spoonful of grapefruit. He's reading the paper but he catches me glancing at him and our eyes catch over the centerpiece bouquet of roses. He lowers the paper slightly, just enough for me to see his smirk, then he snaps it back up and continues to read.

Jackass, I shake my head with a smile. But I know better than to say it aloud. My ass still smarts from last night. I shift on the padded chair he thoughtfully brought out for me for this morning's breakfast.

He's always so thoughtful. Yes, he's also the Master who loves to command my pleasure...but I love that, too. It's something we share. The past few days...our intimacy has gone to levels I didn't even know was possible. I've never felt more connected to another person in my life. If I'd known that two people could...but maybe it takes the *right* person for this kind of magic to happen. And maybe most people don't find it.

My eyes trail over Logan's strong hands and then back up to his face peeking over the top of the paper. I can just make out his eyes. Thank goodness he's taken out those ridiculous contacts. I can see *my* Logan's eyes again. And he hasn't put the mask back on, which I consider a victory. He knows he can be himself with me.

And I know it will take time, but I'll show him that the rest of the world will accept him just like I have. What happened to him was a horrible accident but his scars aren't *that* bad. Okay, they were a little shocking at first, but once you know they're there, they start to just become part of the landscape of his face.

His life story marks his face and it also marks that he survived it and has become so incredibly strong in spite of all that happened to him. I want to show the world his strength. I want to show *him* his strength and that the world can love him just like I d—

I choke on the bite of grapefruit I just took and scramble to reach for my water glass. Not that I lov— I mean, we've barely reconnected, and back in the day it was just a crush. It's not that deep yet, not that intense.

"Daphne!" Logan's already around the table and his hand pounds me on the back. "Are you all right?"

I sputter and hold up a hand. "I'm fine. Fine." I cough again and finally get a long, cool drink of water. Then I push the chair back from the table. Logan jumps out of the way just in time.

"Daphne," he says, his voice half concern, half warning.

"I'm fine." I smile brightly. "I'm just going to get ready

for the day. I cover my mouth and cough into my elbow, then smile again and turn around, bounding out the door.

I've been with him almost 24/7 for the past week and I just need a second. "Just a second," I whisper to myself, huffing a bit of hair out of my face as I lean against the door. Then I cover my hands with my face.

I just haven't had any time to process everything that's happened. There's just experience after experience after experience, with short bouts of heavy sleep in between, ever since I got over my illness last week.

I do a quick count of the nights and days. Shit, has it really been ten days since the ball? So much has happened. I unmasked the Beast, found Logan. Gave my virginity to the man of my dreams, the man I've always loved—

There's that word again. Love. Do I really feel that for Logan? I mean, we made love last night— I cringe and slump against the wall. Because have we really? Have we *made love*? Or is this just more of my naiveté? In Logan's mind, have we just been 'fucking'?

But no, the things he's said to me, it's been more than that, surely...

...says the *virgin*.

Okay, recently devirginized, but still. What do I know about how men work?

He's not 'men', he's *Logan*.

I pace down the hall, arguments churning back and forth in my head. The wood creaks under my frantic steps. I pause at the top of the huge staircase. There's a watery light coming from the first floor—from the front door.

Logan might be okay with me roaming the castle, but he'd probably get weird if I ran out the door. *Because he's a creepy stalker/psycho captor,* whispers the rational part of me.

Yes, but he's my *creepy stalker. And deep down, he's Logan.* Ugh. I wish I had someone to *talk* to about all this.

Rachel. She's the perfect person to talk about boys with. Then I shake my head. There's no way I can tell her about all this.

But thinking about her now, gods, she must be so worried. I haven't talked to her in days.

I pause halfway down the staircase. I'm about to turn and go back up when a familiar looking bag catches my eye. My purse! On the table next to the door. I skip down the rest of the stairs and grab it. Notebook, chapstick, an empty case for the glasses I'm wearing now. The pair Logan gave back to me.

At the bottom of my purse is my charger. My heart starts thumping double-time. Biting my lip, I go to the door. After a moment of hesitation, I push it open. The stoop is empty. There's no phone.

Am I disappointed or relieved? I shut the door. Time to go back to Logan.

But before I grab my purse, something makes me open the side table's drawer. And there's my phone. Its screen is a little cracked and the battery's dead, but I have the charger.

I plug it in. It's been over a week since I've touched base with Rachel. I wince. Yeah, bad friend here. Okay, so for some of that I was super sick, but still. I should have called her as soon as I was better. She must be worried like crazy.

The phone's so super-dead that it takes a few minutes for it to charge even enough to turn on. When it finally does, *beep* after *beep* sounds as messages start pouring in.

RACHEL: HEY BABE, HOW'S VACATION? HAVEN'T HEARD FROM YOU LATELY. LET ME KNOW YOU'RE ALIVE, LOL

RACHEL: Daphne, this isn't funny. Message or call, you're starting to freak me out

RACHEL: Call me right now

RACHEL: I'm serious, bitch, call me or I'm gonna like file a missing person's report. I'm officially freaked.

That was yesterday. Shit! I immediately dial her number.

"Daphne!" she answers, her voice frantic. "Finally!"

"Hey, Rachel."

"I can't believe it's you." Her voice is filled with relief. "Are you okay?"

"I'm okay." I touch the window, tracing the patterns left by frost.

"Are you sure? You just disappeared! I know you said you needed to get away for some research but...what the actual fuck?"

I smile at her choice of words. "I know, Rachel. I know, and I'm sorry. Things have been...difficult."

"I don't know how to handle this. The press is closing in, asking for you. Nobody knows where you are. Adam Archer keeps calling. He even has private detectives looking for you. I'm this close to telling him to go ahead and file the missing person's report."

Shit, Adam. "Don't do that. I'm alive. I'm fine."

"Where are you?"

"I'm staying with...a friend. It's complicated." *Understatement of the century.*

Rachel blows out a frustrated breath. "Okay, then, when are you coming back?"

I shut my eyes, leaning my forehead against the freezing glass. "I don't know. Soon."

"Daphne," her voice is half exasperated employee, half

worried friend. "You gotta come back. The board is livid. I told them you were doing research and also taking time off for your birthday and the anniversary of your mother's death, but they're not buying it. I don't know how much longer I can hold them off."

"Not much longer," I say quickly. *Shit.* I have to get back to New Olympus. Rachel's right—I have too much responsibility. "I promise."

Her voice drops. "It's not just the company. It's your father. He's...not doing well."

Frost slices through me. I stand. "What happened? What's wrong?"

"The nurses don't know. It might be the stress and shock from learning we couldn't reach you—"

"You told him that?" *Fuck!*

"I didn't have a choice! You just disappeared! I didn't know if you were on holiday like you said or dead in a ditch!"

"All right, all right," I soothe. It's not Rachel's fault all this happened. "I understand. I'm sorry. I'll be back—right away. Today. I'll call you back in a few hours." I have to vow several times to call before Rachel lets me end the call. I hang up and drop my phone into my purse.

I don't have any time to waste. There's too much riding on me—my company, the board, Adam's expectations. My father's life. I can't stay here.

I have to convince Logan to let me go.

TWENTY-THREE

Logan

THE DOOR CREAKS open slowly and Daphne enters. She looks nervous, her cheeks flushed. If I had to guess, I'd say my little submissive feels guilty about something.

"Logan, I need to ask you something."

"Yes?" I ask, lazily. I'm feeling magnanimous today. Perhaps I won't punish her too harshly for breaking a rule.

She fidgets. My disobedient little kitten.

She lifts her chin. "I called my assistant."

"You what?" I'm looming over her before I realized I've crossed the room.

She raises her chin and stares me down. "I didn't do anything wrong."

"I'll be the judge of that," I grit out. "We had an agreement when you came here."

Her mouth falls open. "I didn't agree to never contact the outside world! It's my goddamn phone."

"I thought your time in the tower would teach you that

nothing belongs to you. You have no privileges unless I give them to you."

Her mouth falls open. "I thought...we were past all that."

"Is that why you snuck out? To phone her behind my back?"

She flushes. *Busted.* "That's not fair. I have a life. Friends. They were freaking out."

She's going to leave me. "You have no life anymore," I roar. She's changed everything, brought the sun back to my world, and she's going to plunge me back into darkness.

Instead of flinching, she looks at me with pity. Her gaze softens. "Oh, Logan." She cups my face with her hands. "It doesn't have to be this way."

I jerk away. "Yes, it does. You agreed to do as I say. My game, my rules."

She straightens, her hands fisting at her sides. "Your game is fucked up."

"Oh Daphne." My hands close on her arms. "You have no idea."

Daphne

"WHERE ARE YOU TAKING ME?" *Please not the tower.* Why did I think we were back to normal? What evidence did I have that Logan would be rational? He's different, changed. Completely deranged.

When he glares down at me, the blue of his eyes reduced to an icy ring around blown pupils, my heart sinks. Logan is gone. There is only the Beast.

He drags me down a staircase—the opposite direction of the tower—and I sag with relief. Relief that's short lived when he brings me into a cold stone room unlike any I've seen before. My mouth drops open.

A huge wooden X shaped cross dominates the middle of the room along with leather-topped tables, low benches with angled seats. Implements of such shapes and varieties I can't even imagine what they could all be used for.

"What is this place?" I breath.

"My playroom." He leads me to the middle of the room and positions me in front of the cross. I'm too busy gazing numbly at the wall of implements—everything from red handled crops to wooden paddles to wicked looking whips —that I don't try to fight him.

"Play?"

"My sort of play." He turns me to face the cross and cuffs my arms above my head before leaning in to whisper. "Welcome to the dungeon."

BEAST

MY LITTLE SUBMISSIVE SWALLOWS, her eyes wide. "You're crazy."

"I'm not disputing it. You are at my mercy. I think it's time you beg."

"If you want me to beg, I will."

"Not yet." I thrust a rose sideways between her teeth, a makeshift gag. I brought a dozen roses down here in anticipation of showing her this place. This dungeon, these implements, this was another part of my gift to her. I was going to wait until she was stronger to put her through her paces but no.

I need to break her down until she needs me. Craves me. *Will never leave...*

As I peel away her leggings, I get a whiff of her arousal. She wants this as much as I do.

I cut off her shirt and bra, and grab another rose, running it down her back. She naked but for a see-through pair of panties. She shivers, but not from cold. I keep it warm down here. No, she's already falling under my spell.

"Is this what you wanted, Daphne?" I murmur. "To know what I would do to keep you? The lengths I would go?" I run the rose down the cleft of her ass, smirking as she shifts her weight from foot to foot. "You want me to claim you, don't you? Here?" I palm her ass, squeezing gently before giving the firm globe a smack. She jolts against the cross. "Do you need your Master to claim all of you?"

"You're nuts," she breathes, but her accusation holds no heat. I grab a fistful of her thick hair and ease her head back. She's already panting, lips parted, nipples beaded. Her eyes are hooded and I bet if I checked her pussy, she'd be sopping wet.

"Doesn't take much with you, does it?"

"Fuck you."

"Oh, you most certainly will be. Fucked long and hard by me."

Now she's rocking her hips, seeking stimulation against the wooden cross.

"Ah ah," I tsk. Time to turn in my rose for a sterner implement. I braid her hair loosely and tuck it over her shoulder, out of the way. I run my hands up and down her limbs and back, then select a flogger.

"Let's get you warmed up." I snap the flogger, letting

the leather strands rain on her back. Her shoulders immediately relax as she accepts the sensations. The thudding strands give her a massage, with a light sting mixed in.

Her pale limbs are rosy by the time I'm done. And her back is arched, her body rising to meet the flogger.

"Good girl."

She sighs at my praise. I slip a hand between her mons and the cross, finding her smooth folds and stroking them. Her juices coat my fingers.

How can she not realize she was born for this? Made for me? Why is she so quick to throw it away?

I grit my teeth and pull away. She whimpers but doesn't fight when I undo her bindings and lead her to a spanking bench. She bends over willingly, offering up her bottom to my most depraved whims.

I hook my fingers into the side of her panties and jerk outwards, tearing the lace. I let the flimsy scraps fall to the floor. "Count," I order and let my hand fall on her reddened ass. After five, her voice is choked with tears. Her hips wiggle a little but she doesn't try to escape.

And I fall to my knees. "Good girl. You've earned your reward." I tip her over further, baring her sweet cunt to my mouth. I lick up all her juices and probe her ass with my tongue as she squeals.

"You like that, dirty girl?" My cock is a steel bar pressed to the front of my slacks. I rim her dark whorl with the tip of my finger before pressing inside. "Breathe out and bear down," I order, and smack her ass when she doesn't immediately comply. Her tight ass swallows my thick finger and I reward her, tickling her clit until she cums with a cry.

"Fuck me." I can't shuck out of my pants fast enough. Thank gods I had all this furniture custom made for multiple uses. I prop her the way I want her and sink into her hot cunt, pounding her from behind. Her inner muscles flutter as her orgasm goes on and on. "That's it, kitten. Cum on your Master's cock."

I grab a handful of her hair and draw her head back, keeping her back arched. Her little cries are maddening and I roar, slamming my hips into her until the sturdy bench shakes. I fuck her like a wild man. An animal. A Beast.

When I cum and pull out, she's still shaking with aftershocks. I cup her ass, enjoying the heat searing my palm.

"Soon, I will take all of you," I promise as I gather her into my arms. I expect her to flinch and protest—she's gone from virgin to dungeon in a few short days—but she snuggles against me. A happy, sated sub.

"Logan," she murmurs, twining her arms around my neck, bringing me closer to kiss me.

And I'm lost. I could lock her away forever, make her depend on me for food, shelter, human interaction, become her everything, but it wouldn't change the truth.

Without her my life is meaningless.

I need her more than she needs me.

"PLEASE, LOGAN," she whispers softly. "Just hear me out."

I've bathed and fed Daphne, and we're back in the library, in front of the fire. She waited until we were cozy, laughing at old inside jokes, before setting down her hot chocolate and facing me. "I need to go see my father. He's not well."

I rise and go to stand at the mantel. Who told Daphne to speak softly during negotiations? Because it's working. I can't bear to meet her trusting gaze.

"I know you say he did terrible things to you—"

"He did do terrible things." I say to the gilt framed mirror above the fireplace. The reflective surface is old and warped, obscuring my marred face.

"Logan, he's the only father I've got. Please."

"No."

"The old Logan would help me," she murmurs almost to herself. "He had compassion."

"The old Logan is dead. Coded twice, remember?"

She's quiet, but I feel the weight of her gaze on my back. Her hope. I thought it'd be easier when she knew who I was, accepted it. Fuck me, it's not.

"Logan, if there's anything left of the man you were—"

"There isn't." I laugh bitterly. "Because of them."

Soft footfalls on the carpet herald her. She touches my back, urging me to turn.

I almost back away before I remind myself that she's not the predator. I am. But she puts her hands on either side of my face. She doesn't flinch when her soft hands touch marred skin. She looks me right in the eye. "You don't have to be like them."

I'm nothing like them. But when it comes to her, there's no line I won't cross.

"You're staying here," I order, hardening myself. "And that's final."

TWENTY-FOUR

Logan

THE NEXT MORNING, I'm settled by the fire in the library when I hear a door open and close. I'm on my feet, pounding down the hall. She wouldn't just leave, would she?

She's standing in the hall, her head stuck in a closet. "I'm looking for a coat." She pulls out a heavy fur—a leftover from the former owner's wife—and makes a face.

I take the coat from her. "Why?"

"I want to walk in the garden."

"It's too cold."

"Please, Logan."

It's getting harder and harder to say no to her.

"Fine," I mutter. "But the second I think you're too cold and order you back inside, you obey, understand? You're still recovering."

She nods, smiling. And after I've bundled her up and

shrugged on my great coat, I hold out my hand. She takes it, drapes it over her shoulders and tucks herself into my side.

We head out together, braving the bitter cold to view the sad winter garden. She's so small it takes two of her steps to match my long stride. I slow for her benefit, keeping a careful eye on her flushed cheeks. How have I lived so long without her smile? Without her near? Her presence at my side feels so right.

I guide her through the winter garden, pointing out the greenhouse down the hill where I grow tropical plants. I offer to show it to her but she declines, preferring to amble the frosty path, her breath puffing in the freezing air. We reach the part of the hill that overlooks the labyrinth and she studies the maze of tall evergreens.

"Who designed the labyrinth?" she asks.

"I did, years ago. Before I owned the place. I did the one for the Autumnal ball, too."

Her forehead wrinkles. I know she's thinking of that night, our meeting in the maze.

"You know, when you fainted, I first thought it was because you recognized me."

She shakes her head, her gaze still unfocused.

"When you didn't wake, I panicked. Your pupils were dilated."

"I know," she murmurs. "Someone at the ball thought I'd been taking belladonna."

"You had quite a cocktail of drugs in your system." I clench my jaw when I think of it. If I hadn't been there...

She presses her lips together, studying my face. And I know what she's thinking.

"It wasn't me. I would never do that, Daphne."

"Hmmm," she says. But when I turn her to start back to the castle, she doesn't pull away.

"Yet another reason you should stay here," I tell her. "We don't know who tried to drug you. Whether it was an accident or meant for someone else. Or if someone's targeting you..." I make a mental note to check in with my contacts in the city. I sent a private investigator to uncover more about that night, but haven't heard anything. And I've been a little distracted since.

Daphne doesn't protest, doesn't argue, but her steps slow as we reach the frozen terrace. She stops and stares up at the sheer stone face of the castle wall.

"The tallest building," she mumbles.

"What's that?"

"Nothing. Something I read once. A quote by Joseph Campbell: 'If you want to understand what's most important to a society, don't examine its art or literature, simply look at its biggest buildings.'" Her eyes scan the grey-green stone, the towers, the turrets.

"My little homeschool genius." I brush a tendril of hair from her face.

She rolls her eyes at me. "It makes sense. In medieval times, the tallest building in a village was a cathedral. Religion ruled. Then came the political palace."

I study the castle with her. "And a castle? What does that mean?"

She faces me, penetrating me with her fierce green gaze.

"High walls," she says. "An impenetrable stone fortress." She tilts her head. "You don't want to let anyone in."

I straighten her coat and pull her close. "I let you in."

She raises a brow. I can hear her thinking, *yes, as your prisoner. A reluctant guest, at best.*

"Come. It's too cold." I release her and guide her to the

door, a hand on her back. She hesitates on the threshold, and it takes everything I have not to throw her over my shoulder.

I'm putting the coats back into the closet when she says in a low voice, "You think the walls will keep me in. But I'm not the one actually imprisoned here."

"What do you mean?" I take her elbow and steer her to the nearest fireplace. I position her in front of the blaze, but it's not enough. Taking her hand, I start to chafe it.

"When was the last time you left this place? Other than the night of the ball."

"You forget." I drop her right hand and reach for the left. "I waited for you at your mother's grave."

She flushes, bowing her head.

I gentle my tone, really considering her question. "But you're right. Before that, I'd been a year in this place without stepping out the front door. But what about you, Daphne? What's the tallest building in your life?" When she gives no answer, I supply it. "Belladonna. The aptly named. Beautiful woman. Poison."

She sighs. "We help people."

"Is that why your father moved the headquarters to the most expensive area in the city?" I catch her chin. "New Olympus worships power. Money. Greed."

"I don't deny it. Logan, I'm trying to change it. To hold to my ideals. You could help me." For a moment her expression blazes with hope. Then she turns to the fire, shuttering her expression, angling her face away.

And I've never felt more like a monster.

"Daphne."

She turns, her cheeks still pink from the chill. Gods, she's so beautiful. She's more than I deserve.

And I must be crazy because I open my mouth and hear myself saying, "If I let you go, you must promise to return."

She doesn't respond right away. She squints those perfect green eyes, studying me.

"You have to promise," I say raggedly. I'm surprised my chest hasn't cracked down the middle, that I'm not bleeding out in the middle of the frostbitten garden. Because that's how it feels.

She leans into me and I almost stagger with relief. I need her close, always.

"I'm not the one who left and stayed away," she reminds me. She lays her hand on my cheek again, looks me straight in the eye. "I promise."

TWENTY-FIVE

Daphne

THE SAME KINDLY OLD cabbie picks me up in his taxi. If he's curious why he keeps ferrying a young woman back and forth from the city to this castle, he holds his tongue.

Logan stands on the stoop, dark and forbidding in his greatcoat.

"I promise," I mouth. I watch him until the road curves and the castle disappears.

"Oh thank gods," Rachel gasps when I call her. "The board is breathing down my neck. They've been here since practically dawn, holed up in the executive conference room." *Plotting your removal* I hear the end of the sentence she doesn't speak.

"Tell them I'm on my way. I have to make a stop first."

"DAPHNE," my father greets me. He looks thinner than

when I last saw him, but there's a healthier flush to his cheeks. Maybe Rachel was wrong? Maybe he's actually doing better?

"Dad," I kiss his cheek and stand a little ways from the bed. "I need to ask you some things. You're not going to like it but I need to hear the answers."

"Is this about the patents? Because—"

"No. Not exactly." I take a deep breath. S*teady*. "Why didn't you tell me what happened to Logan?"

In a flash, my father grows so pale I jolt with alarm. "Dad?" I take his hand.

"You can't trust him." Eyes wide, he squeezes the life out of my hand. "Daphne, please, promise me you won't ever go near him."

Promise me.

"Dad, you're scaring me. I can't make that promise."

"He's a bad man."

I sigh. I can't really deny that. Good men don't lock women in towers or torture them in dungeons. Even if that torture was delicious...

"I'm a grown woman. I can make my own decisions." Coming here was a mistake. My father is too frail to answer for his past mistakes.

I lean forward and press a kiss to his liver-spotted brow. "Don't worry about me. You just focus on getting better."

"I won't rest easy until I know you're safe."

"I'm safe. I'm here, aren't I? And I'm headed to the office next. I'm going to meet with the board."

"I know. Adam called. He's meeting you there."

I press my lips together. I can't exactly tell my dad I'm going to stop the merger and figure out another way to save Belladonna without selling out to Archer Industries. Even if Adam did half the evil things Logan accused him of, I don't trust him. Logan doesn't trust my dad, either, but I'm sure there's an explanation for my father's actions.

I just can't ask him about it until he gets better.

"Adam will fix everything." Dad pats my hand. "You just listen to him. He'll take care of my girl."

"I don't need anyone to take care of me."

"Nonsense. I told Adam when he called he had my blessing. He's going to make everything right." Dad smiles.

I'm about to ask what he means when the new nurse walks in. "Dr. Laurel?"

"Yes?" My dad and I say at the same time. This time he does laugh. "This is my girl," he tells the nurse proudly. "Youngest recipient of the Avicennius grant. CEO of a top research firm at only twenty-five years old."

"You must be so proud," the nurse coos.

I force a smile to my face. I used to love when my dad talked about me this way. But now I want to make him look in my eyes as I ask: *Am I just a sum of my achievements? Will you ever see the real me?*

No one knows you like I know you, Logan told me. Is this what he meant?

"—time for your medication," the nurse is saying. "Maybe your daughter could come back tomorrow?"

"Of course," I rise, leaning down to kiss my dad's cheek. "I'll be back."

"Daphne," he fumbles with my hand. "I love you."

"Love you, too." *Even if I'm no longer going to live to please you.*

Rachel is waiting in her car to pick me up.

"You're alive." She looks relieved, still perfectly put together in a pink skirt suit.

"I'm alive." The cold surrounds me but I don't feel it. "I have so much to tell you."

"I bet. You look good though," she looks me up and down before turning her attention to the road.

"Thanks. I've been sick, actually, but I rested and I've never felt better." It's true. Being with Logan was like waking from a dream.

"Well, I'm glad you got some time to yourself. I'm sorry I couldn't hold down the fort better than I did. Things are... really crazy right now." There are stress lines on her brow I've never seen before.

"Is Adam waiting for me?"

"Yes. And the press are mobbing the place. They think there's a scandal. And—" She bites her lip.

"What is it?"

"The board is still in closed door talks. I think they're going to vote you out. I'm sorry, I—"

"It's not your fault," I tell her firmly. "I shouldn't have bailed like that. But I had to." I briefly outline what I've found out about Belladonna, including the secret sale of the patents and my meeting with the man who owns them.

"Logan was my father's old business partner. They founded Belladonna together, but they had a falling out and went their separate ways. Logan got my dad to sell the patents at a time when Belladonna was struggling. After my mom's death."

"Crazy," Rachel shakes her head.

"You have no idea," I murmur. Logan did all this under the guise of a different company, one he co-owned with the businessman who willed him the castle. And Logan believes my dad and Adam tried to kill him...

"There's something you're not telling me."

Yeah, all the tantalizing details of my captivity, sexy torture, and first orgasms with the man I've always longed for. I hold her gaze, trying not to blush.

Fortunately Rachel is still trying to wrap her head around the details I have told her. "I can't believe your father sold the patents."

"It happened after my mother's death. He was desperate."

"So what are you going to do? Belladonna's entire net worth is tied up in those patents. If we don't have the rights to develop the research—"

"I've got it figured out," I say and she blinks. I've never sounded so firm before, but I've never been so sure of anything in my life. Belladonna is my company, and I'm going to steer her true. "For the first time in my life, I'm thinking clearly."

"All right," Rachel murmurs, her brow furrowing as she approaches our building. She's right—there are press mobbing the front. I resist the urge to slide down in my seat as we pass them. "I'll drop you off," Rachel says as she pulls around back. "Go get 'em. I'm right behind you."

"Thanks," I shoot her a smile and exit the car. My confident stride lasts until I'm almost to the lobby elevators. A tall man is waiting by reception, wearing a greatcoat. My steps slow when he turns. Smooth skin, blond hair sleekly combed back from his model perfect face. Adam Archer.

I wait, but there are no belly flutters. No excitement at seeing Adam. No, I'm disappointed. Even with his scars, Logan outshines Adam's movie star good looks.

But when Adam sees me, he looks relieved. I feel a twinge of guilt. Weak, but it's there.

"There you are." He catches me in his arms. To my shock, he puts his hands on my cheeks and kisses me full on the mouth.

"Adam," I break away. Guilt totally gone. "What are

you doing?" I want to wipe my lips, it feels so wrong to have felt someone's kiss other than Logan's.

"It'll be all right, Daphne. I talked to your father. I know just what to do."

I scrunch my face, jerking back from Adam. Does he always wear this much cologne?

"Adam, that's...very kind. But I don't need—"

But Adam isn't listening.

"Here she is!" Adam waves to someone behind my head. The elevator has opened and several board members are standing there, scowling at me. A committee of vultures, identical to the man with their glowering faces and dark suits.

"I've got her," Adam says and turns me to face him. "Daphne, are you ready?"

"Ready for what?"

"Our press conference."

"Wait." Everything is happening too fast. "What press conference?"

"Just follow my lead." He's tugging me to the door. The security guards are opening it.

"No—wait—"

Cameras flash. I'm blinded.

"She's here, everyone," Adam is saying, laughing. He shines his toothpaste grin at everyone, basking in the flashing lights. He loves the cameras and they love him.

"Mr. Archer! Mr. Archer!"

"No—" I try to blunder back into the building, but the board is there, waiting just inside. Adam catches my arm and eases me into his side.

"She's a little camera shy. But that's okay. I talk enough for the both of us."

Oh gods, no. I can feel it happening—the old Daphne

surfacing. The people pleaser, the one who does whatever her father tells her to do. *Smile for the camera, Daphne. Hold the award up nice and high so we all can see it. See what you're worth.*

You don't see me. I want to scream. *You never did.* But Adam is waving to a TV crew, his arm around me as we pose. I move with him in lockstep. Everyone's speaking over me and I just let them.

"Dr. Laurel, where were you? Can you comment on the state of the merger?"

"Enough, enough," Adam waves his hands and the press settles down. I've always wondered how he could do that—magically calm the storm. "I have a question to ask Daphne. And I think you'll want to hear it."

My heart beats so loud I barely hear what he says next. But I don't need to. I can guess. Because, in front of everyone, the ecstatic press and the somber-faced board members, Adam gets down on one knee.

No. My heart stops.

"Daphne," Adam murmurs.

What, my lips shape the word but no sound comes out. From his pocket, Adam produces a small black box and opens it. A diamond flashes like a paparazzi's camera.

Over the rising roar of the crowd and the rushing in my ears I read Adam's lips as he asks, "Will you make me the happiest man on Earth?"

TWENTY-SIX

Logan

LETTING her go was the right thing to do. I pace the basement lab while waiting for the latest set of experiments to run.

Work is the only thing I can think to do so I don't go out of my mind while she's gone from the castle. She'll like that I'm doing work on Battleman's. When she gets back I'll finally tell her what I'm working on. Maybe... Maybe we could work on it together. It could be *our* life's goal together. I could prove to her she doesn't have to carry the load alone anymore.

Still, other thoughts pop in, and they're annoyingly loud.

You should never have let her go. The second they get her back in her clutches, she'll—

No. She's not like that. She's strong. I've helped her become strong. She's mine. She swore a sacred vow when she gave her body to me and me alone. They can never have back what's mine.

My hands clench in fists but I force myself to breathe out. She's my Daphne. Loyal to a fault. She's the one person in the world who will never betray me.

But gods, I miss her face already.

I heave my large body down into an office chair in front of a research laptop and in spite of myself, can't help but type her name in a search bar.

I just need to see her face to tide me over. She should be calling any moment. She said she'd keep me up to date on how her father is and when she'll be back. My phone is in my breast pocket but I don't pull it out for the thousandth time to check the battery and whether or not the volume is at full capacity. It's a weakness and I hate that she makes me weak.

But for Daphne, I'll bear a little weakness.

So I pull up the page of results from her name, expecting the same old news articles from years ago with press photos.

But instead—

My fist pounds on the table when the first thing that comes up is a photo of the two of them.

Adam fucking Archer.

Holding my Daphne's hand, grinning up at her with the smile his father paid a fortune for, down on one fucking knee.

The click-bait headline shouts: Magnate Playboy Adam Archer Finally Getting Hitched!

I roar and throw the laptop against the wall, smashing it to pieces. Then I stand and grab anything else within range. Raging. Destroying everything.

When I'm done, almost all the lab equipment is

upended, there's shattered glass everywhere, and my heart is on the floor among the shards.

She was just like the rest of them after all.

A two-faced liar who would've said anything to get away from me. To get back to her *fiancé*. How they're probably laughing at me.

She's made a fool of me.

And the Master is going to make her pay.

EPILOGUE

Daphne

There's an engagement ring on my finger. How the hell did that just happen? I stare down in shock even as the click and flash of a hundred cameras go off, memorializing the moment. One second I was trying to think of how to do damage control and then Adam was down on one knee and then—

Logan. Oh gods. What did I just do? I'm going to be sick.

But Adam's grabbing my hand and holding it up, grinning at all the reporters. I never actually said *yes*. Not the words. I just sort of stared at Adam and gave a head bobble and then he shouted to the crowd that I *did* say yes and put the ring on my finger.

I do my best to keep the horror off my face. How could he do this? How could he put me on the spot like this?

Then I remember: Adam doesn't know. No one knows I've spent the last two weeks falling in l— I mean, becoming extremely close with another man. A man I've let master me. It's not hard to imagine Logan's fury when he finds out about this.

But that's not what's gutting me. It's knowing that underneath his anger and rage, I'll have hurt him. Hurt him so deeply.

No, panic chokes me. No, I'll be able to explain it. I didn't have a choice. If I can just explain it, then he'll have to understand—

Adam pulls me close and mashes his mouth to mine. His tongue tries to invade my mouth but I seal my lips stubbornly shut. I can only be pushed so far. I understand I lose the company if I don't go along with this. I understand it might be the last shock that pushes my father's health over the edge if I don't agree with the farce.

But I can't betray Logan any more than I already have. I turn my face away from Logan and pull back, smiling at the crowd and waving.

"We have business inside now," I call out to the reporters. "Have to share the happy news!" And then I stride as quickly as humanly possible in these damn heels into the Belladonna offices.

"Oh Mama, it was awful," I cry, tears leaking down my cheeks. I sit, legs folded, beside her grave and the beautiful statue of her likeness, just like I used to do by her bedside. Thornfield, my childhood home, looms in the distance like a comforting monument to sameness in the midst of all this change. This small ancestral graveyard is at the east edge of the property.

"I've made a mess of *everything*." I look up at her, beautiful and serene, the sunshine lighting the cold planes of her stone statue. It's nothing like her and yet better than anything else I have. Right now I'm clinging to anything of her I can get. I need her so much right now.

"Adam wanted to talk after the board meeting but I ran away like a coward after a few minutes. He's sincere and nice but he treats me like he's just going to come in and fix everything. Like I can't do anything myself. And gods, maybe I *can't*. Look at how I screwed it all up when I was CEO."

"And when I tried to tell him I couldn't marry him for real, he just said I was exhausted and that he'd take care of everything. Instead of fighting, I said he was right and I was going to go home and sleep. So then I was going to go straight back to Logan's to explain everything but instead I came here."

Thunder rumbles in the distance and clouds cover the sun, casting my mother's beautiful face in shadow. Like she, too, is turning her face away from me, wherever she is in the heavenly fields of paradise.

I bend over her grave, my tears falling and salting the ground. "Please," I beg. "Don't leave me alone. You always knew what to do. You knew how to handle Daddy when he was being impossible and you always made me feel better no matter how bad things got and I—"

"So *now* you show up at your mother's grave."

I choke out in shock at the voice and swing around. Logan! He's standing not five feet behind me. I jump to my feet and start to run towards him when I notice his face.

His features are cruel and angry.

He saw. He saw the news.

When he grabs my hand and holds it up, exposing

Adam's ring still on my finger, I know for sure. He throws my hand away roughly in disgust.

"You lied to me," he spits.

"No, wait, Logan, it's not what you think—" I start but he swiftly cuts me off.

"Are you engaged to Adam fucking Archer?"

"I- I mean, well technically, but not—"

Before I can get another word out, though, Logan's crossed the few feet between us and his hand is at my throat. "Faithless whore," he spits. "Our bed wasn't even cold before you were off spreading your legs for him. I was just practice, I suppose, to break you in like a bitch in heat?"

I slap him. Hard. "You don't know what you're talking about."

His hand at my throat squeezes and he moves so that his face is only an inch from mine. And I can't help it. My body is trained to respond to his dominance. I liquify beneath him. My curves soften to his hard muscle.

And he feels it. For a second, I see a glimmer of Logan, *my* Logan in his glittering blue eyes before they turn back to ice. "Is this how you were with *him*? Did your cunt soften and squirt when *he* touched you?"

He reaches down, roughly shoves up the skirt of my dress, and grabs my crotch. I have to fight my back arching into his touch.

"I ought to slap you again," I grit out through my teeth.

"Is that a yes?" he all but yells, gripping my sex harder as fury flashes in his eyes.

"No one but you has ever touched me there, *Master*!" I yell at him, just as furious. I know it looks bad, but doesn't he have any faith in me? In what we shared together? He wouldn't even let me tell him my side of things!

He just shakes his head at me. "I can't believe a word out of your lying mouth."

I deflate. So that's how it will be. The truth doesn't matter to him. Only his stupid, misguided vendetta. I shove him in the chest. "Then let me go," I shout, rallying again. "If you won't believe me, then there's no point in any of this."

He lets go of me and I stumble back.

"So that's it?" he laughs. "You and Adam Archer ride off into the sunset together? I don't think so, kitten."

I glare at him. "What do you *want* with me, Logan? You won't believe what I have to tell you."

"No." His dark eyes glare right back at me. "I won't ever believe anything that comes out of your lying mouth ever again. But that doesn't mean your debt to me is nearly begun being paid. I am your Master. And *I* get to say when you leave. Not you."

What? What does *that* mean?

"I- I don't understand," I say slowly.

"You will," he says darkly. "You will."

And then he rushes me, picks me up and slings me over his shoulder.

"Where are you taking me?" I squeal, banging on his back with my tiny fists and kicking uselessly. He locks his thick arm around my legs, holding them down, and walks towards Thornfield manor.

"I'm taking you home."

LOGAN AND DAPHNE'S story has only just begun. No matter how far she runs, her path will always lead her back to the stone castle. Back to the Beast.

Pre-Order BEAUTY AND THE THORNS now so you don't miss a thing!

Hungry for more dark romance from Lee and Stasia now?

Find out what happens when Marcus, the king of the criminal underworld who always gets what he wants decides to capture the beautiful, innocent Cora, in his web. He'll give her all that her heart desires. Except for one thing. Her freedom. She's his to keep, and he's never letting her go.

One-click INNOCENCE now!

And for a limited time, get these two exclusive books not available anywhere else ABSOLUTELY FREE when you subscribe to Stasia Black's and Lee Savino's newsletter, ***Daddy's Sweet Girl by Stasia Black*** and ***Royally F*cked by Lee Savino.***

ALSO BY STASIA BLACK

Dark Contemporary Romances

Beauty's Beast

Beauty and the Thorns

Beauty and the Rose

Innocence

Awakening

Queen of the Underworld

Cut So Deep

Break So Soft

Hurt So Good

The Virgin and the Beast: a Beauty and the Beast Tale

Hunter: a Snow White Romance

The Virgin Next Door: a Ménage Romance

Sci-fi Romances

Theirs to Protect

Theirs to Pleasure

Theirs to Wed

Theirs to Defy

Theirs to Ransom

My Alien's Obsession

My Alien's Baby

ALSO BY LEE SAVINO

Lee's books on Amazon

Contemporary romance:

Beauty and the Lumberjacks: a dark reverse harem romance

Her Marine Daddy

Her Dueling Daddies

Royally Fucked - get free at www.leesavino.com

Paranormal & Sci fi romance:

The Alpha Series

The Draekon Series

The Berserker Series

ABOUT STASIA BLACK

STASIA BLACK grew up in Texas, recently spent a freezing five-year stint in Minnesota, and now is happily planted in sunny California, which she will never, ever leave.

She loves writing, reading, listening to podcasts, and has recently taken up biking after a twenty-year sabbatical (and has the bumps and bruises to prove it). She lives with her own personal cheerleader, aka, her handsome husband, and their teenage son. Wow. Typing that makes her feel old. And writing about herself in the third person makes her feel a little like a nutjob, but ahem! Where were we?

Stasia's drawn to romantic stories that don't take the easy way out. She wants to see beneath people's veneer and poke into their dark places, their twisted motives, and their deepest desires. Basically, she wants to create characters that make readers alternately laugh, cry ugly tears, want to toss their kindles across the room, and then declare they have a new FBB (forever book boyfriend).

Join Stasia's Facebook Group for Readers for access to deleted scenes, to chat with me and other fans and also get access to exclusive giveaways:
Stasia's Facebook Reader Group

facebook.com/stasiablackauthor

twitter.com/stasiawritesmut

instagram.com/stasiablackauthor

ABOUT LEE SAVINO

Lee Savino has grandiose goals but most days can't find her wallet or her keys so she just stays at home and writes. While she was studying creative writing at Hollins University, her first manuscript won the Hollins Fiction Prize.

She lives in the USA with her awesome family. You can find her on Facebook in the **Goddess Group** (which you totally should join).

instagram.com/intothedarkromance

Printed in Great Britain
by Amazon